CHERISH YOU SO

BOOKS BY JAN THOMPSON

CITY/COASTAL/BEACH ROMANCE

Seaside Chapel (7 Books)

JanThompson.com/seaside

Savannah Sweethearts (12 Books)

JanThompson.com/savannah

Vacation Sweethearts (8 Books)

JanThompson.com/vacation

ROMANTIC SUSPENSE/THRILLERS

Protector Sweethearts (6 Books)

JanThompson.com/protector

Defender Sweethearts (6 Books)

JanThompson.com/defender

Binary Hackers (4 Books)

JanThompson.com/binary

JanThompson.com/books

CHERISH YOU SO

SAVANNAH SWEETHEARTS
BOOK FIVE

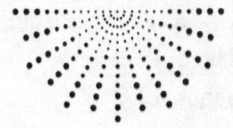

JAN THOMPSON

GEORGIA
PRESS

CHERISH YOU SO (SAVANNAH
SWEETHEARTS BOOK 5)

Book News: JanThompson.com/newsletter
Author Website: JanThompson.com
Published by Georgia Press LLC

This book is a work of fiction. All characters, persons, places,
events, and things are either the product of the author's active
imagination or are used fictitiously.

Scripture taken from the New King James Version®. Copyright
© 1982 by Thomas Nelson. Used by permission. All rights
reserved.

The Savannah College of Art and Design (SCAD) is mentioned
with permission from the university.

eBook ISBN: 978-1-944188-04-7
Paperback ISBN 978-1-944188-29-0

*To my Lord and Savior, Jesus Christ, who died on the
cross to save me from my sins and rose again from the
grave to give me eternal life in heaven.*

*For God so loved the world that He gave His only
begotten Son, that whoever believes in Him should
not perish but have everlasting life.*
—John 3:16

READ A FREE EBOOK IN THE SAME STORY WORLD

Set in Georgia, South Carolina, and Tennessee, this clean and wholesome Christian romance tells the story of art gallery archivist Sheryl Breckenridge and world-famous sculptor Winton Pace. Read this ebook for free!

Time for Me (A Vacation Sweethearts Prequel)
JanThompson.com/time-free

ABOUT THE SAVANNAH SWEETHEARTS SERIES

Welcome to the new south! From *USA Today* bestselling author Jan Thompson come these clean and wholesome, sweet and inspirational Christian romances set in the coastal city of Savannah, Georgia, and on the beaches of Tybee Island by the Atlantic Ocean.

Meet a group of multiracial and multiethnic churchgoing Christians who love the Lord, work hard in their careers, and seek God's will for their love lives. Against a backdrop of ocean, sand, and sun, these inspirational romances showcase aspects of the human need for God and for one another.

Have some tea, settle in a comfortable reading chair, and enjoy these sweet celebrations of faith, hope, and love in Jesus Christ.

SAVANNAH SWEETHEARTS

- Book 1: Ask You Later
- Book 2: Know You More
- Book 3: Tell You Soon
- Book 4: Draw You Near
- Book 5: Cherish You So
- Book 6: Walk You There
- Book 7: Love You Always
- Book 8: Kiss You Now
- Book 9: Find You Again
- Book 10: Wish You Joy
- Book 11: Call You Home
- Book 12: Let You Go

While Savannah Sweethearts books can be read as standalone stories, you can see a bigger picture of the Riverside Chapel community and get a glimpse of the futures of previous characters if you read Books 1-12 in order.

Savannah Sweethearts:
JanThompson.com/sweethearts

For book news, sign up for Jan's mailing list:
JanThompson.com/newsletter

ABOUT CHERISH YOU SO

SAVANNAH SWEETHEARTS BOOK 4

Having come to terms with his disability,
business empire heir Dante Dupree has it all,
but Nadine Saylor is too busy to be impressed
with his accolades, and too busy to fall in love.
Yet, love keeps knocking on her door...

Cherish You So is book 4 in *USA Today* bestselling author Jan Thompson's Savannah Sweethearts series of sweet, clean, and wholesome multiethnic contemporary Christian beach romance celebrating faith, hope, and love in Jesus Christ.

DANTE'S DREAM…

Billionaire bachelor Dante Dupree has arrived.

Managing his paraplegia, he now has a state-of-the-art wheelchair to handle his disability, and a new private jet to take him across the world to buy up smaller companies for his family's Hot Dupree hot sauce empire.

And the best news yet for his career: he has been handpicked to be the next CEO of Hot Dupree, and he's going to inherit a fifth of the multi-billion-dollar family fortune.

He has it all.

At the end of an international business trip, Dante stops in Savannah for merger talks and to visit his pregnant sister, Abilene, now married and living on the beach.

Exuberant and on top of his game, single and free, the center of attention among ladies, and recently voted one of the top ten most eligible young billionaires in the world, self-confident Dante suddenly finds himself in a predicament he cannot solve: he's in love.

But he can't get her attention.

She is not impressed at all with his accolades.

NADINE'S NORMS...

Nadine Saylor is busy, busy, busy.

Her job as a virtual assistant to clients traveling through six or seven time zones keeps her on her toes around the clock.

The last thing she needs right now is Dante Dupree flinging signals and invitations at her, even though he did look handsome in his Lagerfeld tuxedo at his sister's wedding eleven months ago.

Well, that's just on the surface, right?

Nadine keeps telling herself that her calendar is full. There's no room for romance.

Dante can go find someone else to be his Flavor of the Month.

When one of Dante's professional problems intersects with Nadine's personal predicament, they find themselves thrown together to sort out these chapters of their lives.

Does Nadine accept Dante's offer?

Does Dante see Nadine as therapy?

Or are they mistaken?

Shouldn't they find strength in Jesus Christ, who saved their souls?

And has God put them together in this place for such a time as this?

~

Cherish You So (Savannah Sweethearts Book 4):
JanThompson.com/cherish

Savannah Sweethearts:
JanThompson.com/savannah

If you're new to the Savannah Sweethearts series,
the prequel, Ask You Later, is free:
JanThompson.com/ask-free

For book news, subscribe to Jan's mailing list:
JanThompson.com/newsletter

CHERISH YOU SO

CHAPTER ONE

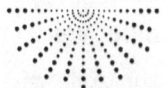

*N*adine Saylor spotted a striped, light-beige tail sticking out of the patch of sea oats. "Bradley!"

The cat ignored her. He continued to chew on the stalks swaying in the summer morning.

Beyond the dunes, a light breeze flitted across Tybee Island, empty at this hour save for residents out and about, jogging or walking.

The day was calm.

But Nadine was not.

"You're going to get sick and throw up all over the place again. You know that. Bradley, come here!"

Nadine stepped closer but didn't leave the sand next to the boardwalk. The sea oats were a protected species, but the law against stomping all over them apparently didn't apply to cats.

Bradley moved farther away from her.

"Come on. I don't have all day." Nadine shook the plastic bag of cat treats in her hand, a poor substitute for natural green leaves. "Come here!"

"Coming!" A male voice resounded over the wash of waves from the Atlantic Ocean.

Nadine spun around—if it was possible on the shifting sand beneath her feet. Her sandals and toes dug into the sand.

Coming over the meandering boardwalk from the beach, Dante Dupree waved at her with one hand as the other pushed one of the hand rims of his wheelchair so casually that it looked like he was heading toward her in slow motion.

His curly hair, much like his sister's, shook in the Atlantic wind. Behind him were the sun and surf, another August day. He looked so fit and so athletic and oh so handso—

Banish the thought!

Nadine blinked before she stared too long at Dante's long arms flexing in the morning sunlight.

Dante was smiling like this was the best day of his life.

"Hi, Nadine." He came to a stop near her. "Need some help?"

He remembers my name.

"Hi, Dante." Saying his name was...interesting.

Here was Dante Dupree, one of the guys whom Nadine had thought she might like to go out with. Once upon a time, that was, until she had found out that he dated numerous women here, there, and everywhere.

Forget about it.

Abilene had told Nadine that those women were dates, nothing serious.

Still, the perception of it bothered Nadine.

I want a gentleman, someone I don't have to hide from Mom and Dad.

Besides, I'm looking for character, not charm.

Nadine straightened up. No reason to make this personal. Just because Abilene had been her best friend—well, until she got married—it didn't mean that the gesture extended to her older brother.

"I didn't know you were out here," Nadine said.

The last time she had seen Dante was at Abilene's wedding back in September. Dante had a flashy date with him, someone who looked like a million-dollar model.

Unlike me.

Dull, uninspiring me.

"Well, you were busy chasing after a cat. I heard you call his name the entire time I was over there." Dante pointed toward the end of the boardwalk. "Too bad the boardwalk doesn't extend far enough."

"Wouldn't that ruin the beach?" Nadine asked.

"I guess."

"Where are your all-terrain wheels?"

"This is all I have." Dante tapped the armrests with the base of his palms.

"Then it's your loss. You know that the Tybee sand is compacted. You could ride a bike on it."

"I live in the landlocked suburbs. I don't need an all-terrain wheelchair. Besides, I don't visit my sister that often. Well, not as often as I should."

Nadine glanced the other way at Abilene's beach house. "Nice house, isn't it?"

"They seem to like it out here," Dante said.

"You're not a beach person? You know, sun, surf, ocean?"

"No." Dante stopped smiling.

His voice was so clipped that it startled Nadine. "Uh, I'm sorry?"

"Don't worry about it. An old memory. Nothing to do with you."

"Well, good." Nadine glanced at her watch. "Anyway, Abilene said you'd be in town, but I didn't know you had already arrived. When did you fly in?"

"I'm two days early, but that's the way to succeed in life, right? Be ahead of the game." Dante lifted his sunglasses, resting them atop his head.

"Game? Life is not a game." Nadine stood

where she was, staring at his steel-colored eyes. They looked...cold.

"Who says it is?" Dante lifted his eyebrows.

"You just did."

"I did?"

"Yes, I heard you."

Dante shrugged. "Figure of speech."

"Every word matters, you know," Nadine said. "God holds us accountable for what comes out of our mouths."

"What about forgiveness?"

"That too. But I'm thinking more of sowing and reaping. Action and consequences."

Whoa.

Nadine had no idea how those words had come out of her mouth. All those years of sitting in church seemed to be paying off.

She wondered how much wiser she could be if she had spent more time in God's Word every day.

Ah... So much to do, so little time. Her clients demanded so much of her.

So tired.

So exhausted.

Nadine sighed. Too loudly, perhaps.

Dante tipped his head slightly. Smiled. "Some unresolved issues there?"

"What do you mean?"

"You've gone philosophical all of a sudden. That

long, silent pause." Dante waved his hands at her. "I can see right clear through it. And here I am, thinking all you're trying to do is retrieve Abilene's cat from destroying the sea oats."

"Cat? Uh-oh." Nadine spun around. "Bradley, where are you?"

She paced back and forth, shaking the treat bag again. It was a useless exercise.

Abilene's cat was nowhere to be found.

"No. No. No." Nadine's heart sank. "What am I going to tell Abilene when she comes home from work?"

Dante chuckled. His wheelchair inched toward the edge of the boardwalk. He was only a few feet away from Nadine.

Too close!

Nadine lost her train of thought.

CHAPTER TWO

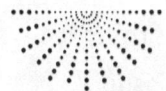

*I*t made Nadine slightly uncomfortable to be this close to a man she had watched from afar for a couple of years, and then some. After having listened to all those complaints Abilene had of her older brother and his pick-and-choose Christianity, Nadine had lost interest in him.

Dante's presence now threatened to revive Nadine's thoughts of Dante, but those thoughts vanished when Nadine remembered the type of man he was.

Dante's eyes were on Nadine. "Bradley is a cat. He'll come home when he wants."

"Huh?"

"Bradley the cat?"

"Oh, yeah." Nadine shook her head. "I

should've known he'd run out the door as soon as I opened it. He needs to stay indoors."

"Why?"

"We don't want him eating rats and birds and such, you know." Nadine called Bradley's name again, each time her voice wavering. She was about to give up. "The last thing we want is for Abilene to be exposed to toxoplasma."

"So that's why you're in charge of cat litter."

"Uh-huh."

"Why can't Lars handle it?"

"Well, Abilene says he makes a—oops. I shouldn't disclose that."

"I already know he makes a mess," Dante said. "Lars leaves crumbs everywhere when he makes a sandwich. I wouldn't be surprised if he leaves a trail of cat litter when he changes the box."

"You're assuming."

Before Dante could reply, several pings pricked the air between them. "One sec. I have to get these."

Nadine watched him check his iPhone. Suddenly aware of the warming sun, she knew her time was up. She had changed the cat litter, accidentally let him escape the big house, and had lost at least forty minutes.

She walked away from Dante, calling out to Bradley.

The cat didn't come.

"Maybe if we go back to the house, he'll come after us," Dante suggested.

"Sure. I could leave the terrace door open."

"I don't want it open," Dante said. "Dad and I are staying here all week. I want the AC on."

"Your dad? I didn't see anyone else this morning."

"He's on his way here." Dante smiled broadly. Charming. "Looks like you and I will see more of each other. How often do you come here?"

"Every day." Nadine laughed. "I'll try to stay out of your way."

"Is that a nervous laugh?" Dante asked.

"What? No. I'm not nervous." *Yes, I am.*

Nadine started walking back toward the house. What a predicament. She had to leave now and go back to work. But shouldn't she wait for Bradley to come home? She'd have to check him for fleas and such. She didn't want Abilene to be bitten by fleas.

Nadine chided herself for not having brought her laptop, considering she might have to wait for Bradley to finish walking among the oats.

She glanced at her watch.

Yikes.

She really, really had to start work for the day. Eight clients wanting pounds of flesh from her. A ninth client traveling through Europe wanted her to proofread his talking points for his speaking engagements in Spain and Portugal. She'd be up all night tonight keeping up with him and his morning speeches.

And the previous night, she had only gotten three hours of sleep.

So tired.

So, so tired.

Dante was right beside her. His eyes seemed to be on his iPhone, which kept pinging.

"Say, do you want me to push you?" Nadine asked. "That way you can check your iPhone hands-free."

"Push me?" Dante lifted both eyebrows. Again. He seemed to do that a lot.

And why am I noticing it?

"No. I don't want to be *pushed*," Dante added. He pointed to some accessories on the wheelchair armrest. "I have a phone dock I'm not using. I'm holding the phone to my ear because I don't want you to hear the rest of the conversation. It's business."

"I'm sorry."

Dante nodded, as if he accepted the apology. "I can take care of myself, thank you very much."

"Sorry. Did I offend you?" Nadine felt bad.

Dante stopped. "Nadine."

Nadine faced him.

"Stop saying you're sorry."

"But I am."

Dante's eyes softened. "I should be the one apologizing. I'm receiving some frustrating emails and messages, and I snapped at you when it has nothing to do with you. If you want to assist me, go ahead, but you might want to save your energy for the cat."

They reached the terrace, and there was Bradley, throwing up under a lounge chair.

"Bradley! Didn't I tell you so?" Nadine shook her finger at the cat, who looked pathetically remorseful.

She'd have to clean up that clump of green grass vomit.

Meanwhile, Bradley let her reach for him. Nadine picked him up, put him in the house, and shut the door. She stared at the mess on the terra-cotta tiles.

"I would offer to help, but I have to make a bunch of calls," Dante said.

"Sure."

"What's that supposed to mean?"

"Huh?"

"You said *sure*. Is that a joke, or is there an underlying meaning to that word?"

"You lost me there, Dante. What are you talking about?"

"Gotcha. What you said earlier. 'Every word

matters.' And 'God holds us accountable for what comes out of our mouths.' Your exact words."

Scary.

"Can't believe you remembered that." Nadine felt a strain on her shoulders.

"I try to remember important things."

Important things?

Nadine didn't think what she had said was all that important. But she had been right.

Words mattered. Words like *tired.*

Exhausted.

And lonely.

CHAPTER THREE

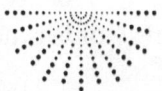

When Dante came back to the terrace, Nadine had finished cleaning up the terra-cotta tiles, and Bradley was sitting on her lap. She was combing his fur with a brush. Her other hand was thumbing her iPhone. She seemed oblivious to his presence at the door.

He watched her hair swirl in the morning breeze, dancing to the tune of the waves.

A couple of seagulls squawked overhead. Distant voices of people on the beach this August weekend told Dante that he should have been on vacation instead of scheduling a merger meeting.

Well, it saved time if he didn't have to make a second trip to Savannah on Thursday. He could easily kill two days by working on his laptop between the fundraising gala on Monday night and the merger meeting on Thursday.

He texted Chelsea again. He reminded her to bring an extra carton of Hot Dupree from the warehouse Monday morning. He figured that if he saw anyone interesting at the gala, he could give them free hot sauce, courtesy of Grandma Dupree, whom everybody knew.

He wondered how long Grandma Dupree was going to last. She had been determined to live past her one-hundredth birthday this November. To keep herself busy, she had been working on another flavor of sauce—a variation of the old, really—which she planned to name after her new great-grandchild.

It was too early to find out the gender of the baby, but Grandma Dupree was all set. The unveiling of the new flavor would be in Savannah in February, when Abilene's baby would be about a month old.

And yes, Dante had to come back for the birth and celebration of his new niece or nephew. If it were a girl, he wouldn't be surprised if his sister named her child Marguerite, Grandma's first name.

He prayed all would be well with his sister's pregnancy.

He tried not to be alarmed that Abilene had a cat in the house, but her obstetrician had said no one needed to worry. As long as Abilene didn't touch the cat litter, and the cat stayed indoors as much as possible, they could keep the toxoplasma parasites to a minimum.

And that was why Nadine was here.

Speaking of whom, Nadine was looking at him now, even as she continued to brush and stroke Bradley's fur.

"You're a good friend." Dante wheeled toward Nadine's lounge chair. His back faced the terrace pillars, the dunes, sand, ocean. He felt the morning sun on his bare neck just above the collar line of his old tee shirt.

"Abilene would do the same for me," Nadine said.

"Good friends are hard to come by."

Nadine nodded.

Bradley purred, rolled on his back, and seemed to want to have his tummy rubbed.

Dante had never seen anyone look so happy, so blissful, sitting in a chair with someone else's cat. Well, besides Grandma Dupree. She had a cat once, a Persian that had died a few years back.

"Do you have a cat?" Dante asked.

"No, but I want to. When I get settled down, I'll rescue some cats."

"Do you have lots of windows?"

"Yeah. A few."

"Grandma's cat loved sunshine. Apple was always looking for slivers of sunlight."

Nadine was silent.

Dante could see her face turning slightly pink. "Are you okay?"

Nadine nodded. "So the cat is gone?"

"A few years ago. Grandma never got another one. She'd outlived all her cats, but she wasn't sure if she could outlive another one."

Dante watched Nadine. Something in her face told him that she had a soft spot for cats.

"Abilene says she's pushing a hundred," Nadine said.

Dante nodded. "Yep. We're having a big birthday bash in New Orleans. And later, here in Savannah, the unveiling of a new hot sauce flavor, of course. Maybe you can come."

"I'll think about it." Nadine's voice lowered. "Must be nice to have a big family."

"There are only three of us siblings, as you know, but we have lots of cousins and nieces and nephews. Too many, perhaps."

"One can never have too much family."

"You?" Dante's iPhone pinged again.

Nadine seemed to ignore his question. "Work beckons!"

On that note, Bradley leapt off her lap. Nadine reached for him. "Don't run off again!"

Dante's long arms reached out, scooped up Bradley, and handed him over to Nadine.

"Let's put him inside," Nadine said. "I have to run. Have a long day ahead."

"We should get a leash," Dante suggested as he followed Nadine into the house.

"Yeah, right." Nadine put canned food into Bradley's dish and fresh water into his bowl. "Have you ever seen a cat on a leash?"

"On Facebook." Dante saw her to the front door.

"You don't have to follow me around," Nadine said. "I've been here before."

Dante still opened the front door for her. "Can't believe my sister made you come here every day."

"I volunteered." Nadine fished for her car key. "It's only for five more months."

"Is she paying you for this?"

"I don't want to be paid. What are friends for?"

Ping! Ping!

Dante frowned at his iPhone. Bad timing! He was trying to chat up a pretty girl. Annoyed, he checked the text message.

Irony of ironies. "Say, Nadine?"

"Yes?" One leg in the car, Nadine stopped.

"You free Monday night?"

"Why?"

"My date can't make it to the gala. Would you accompany me?"

CHAPTER FOUR

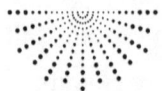

"*N*o. Sorry." Nadine knew her voice was curt, but what Dante had asked irritated her. "I'm busy on Monday."

Dante wheeled closer to the driver's side before she could close the car door.

"It's at night," he reminded her.

"I'm busy at night too."

"Don't tell me you work night and day."

"Pretty much around the clock, whenever I'm needed."

"Don't you ever sleep?"

"When I can. My clients are in different time zones. They don't get a day off, I don't get a day off. I can't go anywhere. Don't you have a bevy of pretty girls to call?"

"Nobody turns me down."

Nadine chuckled. "I just did."

"It's a big to-do. You'll be all over the papers. Visibility for your Saylor Virtual Services?"

He remembers my company.

Has Abilene been talking too much about me to him?

"I'm so busy I can't take on new clients at this time." She pointed to her car door. "Excuse me, Dante. You're kinda blocking my door here. I need to go home, get to work. I'm sure you have work to do too."

"Yeah. Sure. One question?"

"You mean one more question?"

"Would you have said *yes* to the gala if you had known me better?" Dante asked.

Nadine wondered how to respond, how to put it in such a way that he wouldn't see that, yes, she had felt a slight attraction to him, but no, she wasn't about to fill in for his missing date just because she was conveniently there.

"It's because I know that—uh, no." Nadine pursed her lips. "I'm just busy, okay?"

"Know what, Nadine?" Dante pressed. "What's in the press? Social media? Don't believe everything you see or read."

"What about—never mind." She couldn't implicate his sister.

Abilene hadn't told her things about Dante to

gossip. She had been venting and getting all upset, but it was in private conversations.

Nadine and Abilene had always treated each other like sisters and confidants. No way was Nadine going to break that confidence now.

"Let me go, Dante. I have to get to work."

He stepped back. "Okay. If you change your mind, let me know by Sunday."

"If not, you go alone?"

"No, ma'am. Like you said, I have 'a bevy of pretty girls to call.'"

We'll never get along.

He remembers my every word and uses it against me.

Somehow that grated at Nadine. She didn't know why she had these mixed feelings about Dante.

One minute she had enjoyed talking with him. The next minute, she had felt offended when he asked her to accompany him to a gala.

Perhaps his invitation had come across as flippant.

Yep. That's it.

Seething, she could barely look out the windshield as she backed the car out of the driveway.

Dante was still watching her from the driveway. His hands were crossed in front of him, hugging his chest.

Something was on his mind, and Nadine prayed it had nothing to do with her.

She didn't want to cause problems between Dante and his sister. Abilene had been her best friend for a while, and she didn't want to be the source of any rift in the Dupree family.

By the time Nadine arrived at her house some fifty minutes later, she had cooled off.

She parked her car on the cracked driveway. When she had bought this house, her plan had been to get her car into the one-car garage.

Yeah, best-laid plans.

Two years later, half her garage was still filled with packing boxes with books from college and a bunch of junk she hadn't thrown out.

She had no time.

"I still have no time," Nadine said to no one as she locked her car.

She had sufficiently calmed down and was ready to get to work. But as she unlocked her front door and opened it, she remembered Dante's face at Abilene's front door, how he had looked at her with that dashing—

He's not on my radar.

He can't be.

Abilene had told her a few times before how concerned she had been that her brother, close to thirty-three years old, hadn't settled down. He had a new girlfriend every month. A new date on every continent.

Nadine wondered what he did with all those women.

No way am I going to be another flavor of the month.

CHAPTER FIVE

*N*adine could not believe what she was hearing on her phone.

"Mom, why are you doing this?" Her eyes hurt something fierce. She blinked.

Mom droned on. Something about being tired of everything.

"But. But y'all are so—I don't get it, Mom."

Nadine pressed her fingers to her temple. She dragged herself out to the back porch for some fresh air. The screen door slammed shut behind her.

The noonday temperature was pushing a sweaty ninety degrees. Her flip-flops stuck to the stone path as she paced all the way to the wooden fence and then back again to her little house.

"So where are you moving to?" Nadine wiped tears on the back of her hand.

"Cancun," Mom said. "Come see me there, sweetheart."

"Cancun? That feels far away, Mom. Why?"

Nadine sat on the stone steps of her porch. The shade from the roof only extended to her thighs. Her calves and feet were getting hot in the August heat.

"A change of scenery." Mom sounded excited. Almost relieved, Nadine thought.

"Is Dad seeing someone else?" Nadine asked. Her parents had fought for twenty years or more, but never once had Mom followed through on her threats to move out.

"You know your father would never do that," Mom said.

"Then what's the problem?"

"I'm tired of fighting all the time over every little thing. Dinner, for example." Mom rambled on about how argumentative Dad was.

That, he was. Yet, interestingly, Dad rarely argued with Nadine.

Only with Mom.

Still, all Nadine wanted to hear was that Dad had been faithful to Mom. This latest fight had been over burned spaghetti. That was all.

Burned dinner! "Is that all, Mom? Burned dinner?"

Whew. What a relief.

Not!

Her parents had a penchant for blowing everything out of proportion. Dad's claim to fame was that he could find ten different ways of looking at the same thing, and he would hash out each view, regardless of whether anyone cared.

"Mom, this is a very bad time."

"It is."

"I mean, right now. When I have three clients I'm going to lose if I don't get back to work, it stresses me out to hear that you and Dad aren't getting along." *Again.*

"I'm sorry. I didn't mean to put it on you."

"No, don't worry about it. We'll get through this."

"Of course. We always do."

"Why don't I call you tonight when everyone has calmed down?" Nadine went back inside her house. Her stomach rumbled.

"Don't worry about us, sweetheart. We're adults."

Yeah. Adults who fight like kids. "We'll sort this out, Mom."

"We've already sorted it out. We're going to sell the house and split the profits."

It seemed so final.

Nadine decided she had to call Dad to hear his side of the burned-dinner episode.

"Okay. Take care, Nadine. I'll send you a post-card from Cancun."

"All right, Mom. I'll call you tonight." She opened the refrigerator. Found some cold turkey bacon, a chunk of Swiss cheese, and some gluten-free bread. "Go out for dinner or something."

"Dinner?"

"Don't cook tonight. You guys burned dinner last night, right? Thursday night?"

"Not last night, sweetheart. Last Thursday night. I'm at the Miami airport, waiting for my connecting flight to Cancun."

Nadine dropped the glass container on the floor. It shattered.

"What's that noise, sweetheart?" Mom asked. "Are you okay?"

"N-nothing, Mom." Nadine sniffed. "So where did you go after you left Dad?"

"Your aunt Edna's."

Nadine was surprised that Aunt Edna hadn't talked Mom into returning home to Dad. "Listen. Don't do anything rash. We'll pick this up tomorrow morning, okay?"

That should give Nadine enough berth to get Epstein, Jurgen, and Waddell taken care of. Then she'd sit down and pray about how to mediate this latest dispute between her parents.

Over burned dinner, no less!

A week ago!

Why did they wait this long to tell me?

She said goodbye to Mom, hung up, and wept at the kitchen table.

"Lord Jesus, You see all things. I know You saw that coming. Why didn't You stop it?" Immediately, Nadine chided herself. "Forgive me, Lord. I know. I know! If I had *studied up*, I would have been better prepared for this. Your Word would have guided me."

She wondered what refreshing Bible verses she could have recited to Mom had she memorized Scripture as Pastor Flores had urged the congregation of Riverside Chapel to do.

Only one verse came to mind. She had already learned II Corinthians 5:7. It had been years, it seemed, that she had come to know this verse.

For we walk by faith, not by sight.

Over and over, God had chosen to apply it to various parts of her life, from her awkward childhood to her high school years, through college and work life, and now in the company she owned.

"For we walk by faith, not by sight." She said it aloud several times.

"Lord, help me walk by faith in You, and not by sight in the mess I see in my parents' marriage. Thank You, Lord Jesus, that You are faithful and true, even when we mess up."

CHAPTER SIX

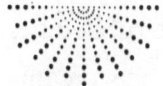

*E*ven from here, Dante could tell that Nadine had been crying. Those red eyes weren't there this morning when he had seen her outside looking for Bradley the cat.

Now, sitting alone in that corner booth at Piper's Place, with her laptop in front of her, she looked somewhat sad.

No one that pretty should look so sad.

Behind Dante, Abilene and Dad were chatting about something funny. Abilene must not have noticed Nadine.

Dad had arrived late morning, skipped lunch, and then he and Dante had driven to River Street to visit Simon's Gallery, now owned by Abilene and Lars.

Abilene had been so vocal about her terrible

JAN THOMPSON

craving for a hot fudge sundae that Dante and Dad
had given in. So here they were at Piper's Place,
standing in line at three o'clock in the afternoon,
looking for a sugar fix.

"Abilene," Dante said.

Abilene and Dad looked his way.

"Yeah?" Abilene rubbed her tummy.

"What kind of ice cream does Nadine like?"
Dante asked.

"Nadine? Why are you asking about her?"

Dante pointed to Nadine's booth. "Just
wondering about her preference."

"Oh." Abilene grinned. "And what are you
going to do with the info?"

By now Dad was laughing.

"I thought she might like to join us," Dante
managed.

"Uh-huh. Seeing that she's not even looking up,
and she's typing away furiously, I'm gathering that
she's busy working. The Nadine I know wouldn't
want to join us at this time. Try again another day,
big Brother."

Dante couldn't believe Abilene wouldn't
help him.

"Get me the usual, will you?" Dante wheeled
away. "Two scoops. Chocolate with chopped
walnuts on top."

"Where are you going?"

"To say hello to a friend."

"Friend?" Abilene gave him an odd look. Her eyes flitted back and forth between her brother and Nadine. "Since when?"

"Since this morning. Thanks to your cat, by the way." And then he was off.

A bundle of nerves formed in his chest. He was surprised, really. He'd never been this nervous in his life. He had traveled the world, signed deals, sold hot sauce to anyone he could find, and never once—not once—had he felt this nervous.

He was at the booth before Nadine noticed him there.

"Hi, Dante. Whatcha doing here?" Nadine asked.

Her nose was still red.

"Having ice cream with Abilene and Dad. Want to join us?" Dante asked as casually as he could.

"No, thanks. I'm busy."

"Busy being sad?" As soon as the question—statement, really—left his lips, Dante wanted to reel it back. Too late.

Nadine's eyes glistened.

"If you need to talk..."

"I'm fine. Thank you. Have an extra scoop for me, okay? I need to get back to work. Thanks for stopping by."

"Okay." Dante decided he would begin praying

for her. "I'll see you tomorrow, then, when you come over to scoop the poop."

Nadine chuckled. "You're a hoot."

"That almost rhymes." Dante didn't leave. "I've been looking at some all-terrain wheels online. Someday, would you have a picnic with me on the beach?"

"Maybe..."

It was good enough for Dante. "Too bad we can't go on a picnic anytime soon."

"How long are you in town?"

"Until next Saturday."

"I'm busy all week anyway," Nadine added.

"Except in the early hours of the morning when you do your cat litter duty."

"Meaning what?" Nadine asked.

"Meaning we can have a breakfast picnic on Abilene's terrace if that's more convenient for you."

"Wouldn't that be kind of odd?"

"Odd? How?" Dante couldn't see it.

"You and I having *breakfast* together?"

"It would be cooler outside."

"Yeah, but what would people say?"

"I don't care what people say."

"Well..." Nadine paused. "You do have a point. There's nothing going on between us. Nothing to talk about."

Somehow Dante wanted that to change.

And yet...

Rushing things to get a date before he went home to New Orleans seemed a bit discourteous.

Perhaps dishonoring, at worst, and disrespectful, at the very least.

The last thing he wanted to do was to dishonor or disrespect Nadine.

CHAPTER SEVEN

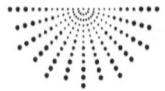

"*S*he can't do this to me right in the middle of our merger talks, Phil. You tell her." At the edge of the pool, Dante was fuming.

Above him, the ten o'clock sun beat down on his bare chest. He had changed into his swimming trunks, ready for a swim in Abilene's pool, when his vice president of operations had called him with the bad news.

As he listened on the speakerphone, his anger rose. Somewhere in the conversation, he realized that Phil didn't care that his assistant of several years had left Hot Dupree, Inc.

"Have I not paid her enough? Ask her what she wants." At the back of his mind, Dante knew that he had lost Chelsea.

Where in the world was he going to find an able
assistant on such short notice?

"Sir, with all due respect, you can't ask her to name the price," Phil said.

"Why not? I did before. No one else has resigned from the company this year. I pay them well." Even as he said that, Dante realized that some of his employees' loyalty was to the dollar, not to any Dupree. Dad had mentioned something to that effect to him before, but he had brushed it off.

Dante wasn't about to admit it had been a mistake to buy Chelsea's loyalty. He wondered if someone else had made her a better offer.

"Look into this, Phil. I want to know why Chelsea's left us right now. The timing is odd."

"And mysterious."

"I don't know about it being mysterious, but it certainly raises some suspicions. Let me know what you find."

As he was talking, he heard the sliding door open behind him. He didn't need to spin around to check who it was. It was either Waylon, his security guard, or Abilene, who hadn't been feeling well at breakfast this morning.

It couldn't be Dad. He had left early to play golf.

As for Dante, he could never play golf again. All because of that irreversible injury.

He would never walk again this side of heaven, never run to the end zone again, and never dance again.

I wonder if Nadine dances.

Nadine?

Why am I thinking of her?

"Sir?"

"Yes, Phil?" Dante sucked in a deep breath. No point thinking about what could never be.

Here was his new normal, as it had been for years. He had to make the best of it.

"Personnel gave me some names. Do you want me to start interviewing, sir?"

"Yeah. Make a short list. You know my requirements." *My demands.*

Dante let him go. He was still upset when he ordered Siri to hang up the call on his iPhone. He pushed another button, and the docking station, together with his charging iPhone, disappeared into the side of his wheelchair.

He sure liked this wheelchair. It had been custom built just for him. Most of all, he liked the Wi-Fi, though he hated to check his emails on his laptop while he sat in his wheelchair. He didn't want to be confined to his wheelchair.

In fact, he wanted to get up and run free.

Something impossible.

"Problem at work?" It was Abilene's voice.

Dante looked up. He had been so absorbed he hadn't noticed the shadow over him. Abilene blocked the sun, but only some.

"You know my assistant, Chelsea?" Dante asked.

"Yeah?"

"I lost her today. She's supposed to be flying in Monday. She quit by email an hour ago. No reason."

"So sorry." Abilene threw down her towel.

Dante thought her belly was huge at four months. It was a bit strange for him to see his baby sister all pregnant. He could envision her married, but Abilene with child? It would take some getting used to.

He would be an uncle for the third time.

Yep, always an uncle, never a father.

The doctors had told him it would take more effort for him to have his own children.

What?

Dante frowned. He couldn't believe the thoughts that had been bouncing around his head this morning.

Maybe he needed more rest. That fitful sleep he had last night hadn't helped. For some reason he couldn't turn this way or that, as he had done before. Although he usually slept on his back, this time he had tried a side position and had woken up sore.

Lord, I wish I could walk again.

Heaven came to his mind.

"There must be a reason she left." Abilene poured sunblock on her arms. "Want some?"

Dante opened up a palm. Abilene squirted some of the lotion on it.

"I don't get it. I pay her three—maybe four—times as much as other CEOs' assistants."

"Maybe she has another income stream," Abilene suggested. "Is she married?"

"No. Boyfriend maybe." Dante slopped sunblock up and down his arms, neck, and shoulders. He didn't burn easily, taking after Dad, but one never knew with those ultraviolet rays. Mom had always been a bit neurotic about making sure the Dupree kids had some sort of sunscreen on before they went outside.

Ironically, after all that, the person who usually got sunburned first was none other than Mom, and almost always on her fair complexioned nose and cheeks. Poor Mom.

"Do you want to find out why your assistant left?" Abilene asked.

Huh? Oh. "I asked Phil to look into it."

Abilene laughed. "Phil, your VP?"

"Why are you laughing?"

"Do you want me to get someone to look into Phil too?"

It was Dante's turn to laugh. "Great. You're saying I'm surrounded by incompetent people."

"You told me that your assistant has great access to your personal data on your laptop. Combine that with untrustworthiness, and you got trouble, big Brother."

"Well..."

"Nobody you have on your payroll right now is loyal to you." Abilene seemed to be on a roll. "They're only loyal to their paychecks."

As I had thought.

"Have you been talking to Dad?" Dante asked.

"I know a lot of things without Dad's help. But right now, only one thing is important. If we don't get in the pool, it's only going to get hotter. A hundred degrees this afternoon, if you can believe it."

Abilene stepped down the ladder into the pool. "Ha. Beat you to it, big Brother!"

CHAPTER EIGHT

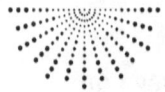

"Watch this!" With his upper-body strength, Dante stretched out his arms and launched himself out of his wheelchair into the pool. It made a spectacular splash and entertained Abilene to no end.

It was a far cry from his first year of intensive rehabilitation after that high school football game that had changed his life. As a wide receiver, he had caught the football and was running for a touchdown when he was tackled from behind. Hundreds of pounds of bodies toppled onto him.

He had heard a sharp snap, and that was all it had taken.

He remembered lying there in the end zone—the football having popped out of his hand—and being unable to move.

At all.

He could still see it, hear it, feel it all. People shouting, yelling, losing it all around him. And his coach crying. It had been a sight to see Coach Sheldon crying in front of the entire high school stadium filled with fans.

And that was that.

Dante had replayed that episode of his life so many times in the last sixteen years that he didn't want to remember it anymore.

It had taken years before he could watch another football game on television.

Well, it hadn't stopped his college plans, but it had sure made it harder to implement them. Yes, he had graduated from Wharton Business School with honors, but what wouldn't he give to be able to walk to the refrigerator on his own two feet to get a can of soda?

Many times he had wondered if he would have been better off dead.

"Catch!" Abilene threw him a float.

Treading water with his arms, Dante reached for the float with one hand. His sister seemed happy as she swam around him.

No, it wouldn't have been better.

Abilene would cry the rest of her life if he had died.

Maybe she was why God had allowed Dante to

live.

"I love you so much, Abilene, my only sister."

"You say that all the time. Why now?" Abilene swam toward him. "Listen. Don't worry about Chelsea. There is a reason she left. We'll get to the bottom of it."

"I'm the future CEO. I can take care of my own personnel."

"I'm a shareholder. I want the company to succeed."

"I hear you, Abilene. Okay. You know someone you can trust, someone outside Hot Dupree, preferably someone Phil doesn't know, who can look into why Chelsea quit so abruptly?"

Abilene nodded. "Ming Wei. He's a PI."

"You trust him because?"

"He looked into Lars. And Nadine trusts him."

"Nadine?"

"I trust whoever Nadine trusts. She's a good judge of character."

"She doesn't trust me." Dante wasn't sure why he blurted that. "Uh..."

Abilene laughed again. "Improve your character and we'll see."

"Improve my character? I have impeccable character."

"If you have to tell me..."

"What's that supposed to mean?"

"Stop dating all those girls."

"I'm not really dating them. They're for the press. Publicity."

"It looks like you're playing the field."

"And that affects Nadine's perception of me?"

"Anyone's perception of you."

"And you?" It had always mattered to Dante what his sister thought of him, but now more so than ever, because she had mentioned Nadine.

Since Nadine had left the house after taking care of Bradley yesterday, she had been on Dante's mind.

He hadn't been too happy that Abilene had texted Nadine to say that Dad was going to scoop the litter all week and that Nadine didn't have to come to the house as long as Dad was in town.

Sigh.

"About your friend, Nadine," Dante said. "Why was she crying at Piper's yesterday afternoon?"

"You want to know because..."

"Curious, is all." Dante hung on to the float.

All around the pool were sounds of Tybee Island, the seabirds and the ocean waves beyond the fence, and the occasional airplane above them.

Dante waited as patiently as he could for his sister to respond. He didn't want her to think he had designs on her best friend. At the same time, his curiosity had intensified on Friday when he had interacted with Nadine twice in the same day.

Abilene swam nearer. "Curious or interested?"

"Maybe both?" Dante had sensed that there was a lot more to Nadine than her polite smiles and chats with him. "Is she dating anyone?"

"Not at the moment. She's super busy, I can tell you that. She works in six or seven different time zones. No time for a boyfriend."

"That busy."

"Yep. Says she has to save up enough in case she has to live alone the rest of her life and support her parents."

"Self-sufficient. I like that."

Abilene stepped up the ladder. "But she's not your type, Dante. So don't bother."

"Not my type?"

"Nope." Abilene swung the pool lift arm over the side of the pool and pushed a button to lower the seat into the water.

"Why do you say that?" Dante shimmied himself into the seat.

"She prefers guys who are homebodies."

"That so."

"Uh-huh. She's nice to everyone, but there are only certain guys she would date."

Abilene pushed a button to lift him out of the

pool. She pushed his wheelchair as close as possible to him, and locked the wheels in place.

"Homebodies don't get anywhere. Don't do anything. Underachievers. What does she see in them?"

Abilene chuckled. "Jealous?"

"No." He'd said it too quickly. "Curious. That's all."

"You said that." Abilene gave him the look. It was a signature Grandma Dupree look: a slight upturn of one eyebrow.

"The homebodies Nadine wants are those who don't travel much. She gets airsick when she flies. She doesn't like long drives. She made one trip last year to see some relatives on the West Coast. That's as far as she goes."

"She flew?" That made Dante curious.

"Yes. Only because a train would take longer, and she had very little vacation time. But she was sick there and back."

"Thanks. Good to know." *Don't want her throwing up all over my Gulfstream.*

Dante transferred himself from the lift onto his wheelchair. He was out of the water, but his heart sank, as if to the bottom of the pool.

There are only certain guys she would date.

Dante glanced at his sister. She was drying her hair, wrapping a beach towel around it.

No need to ask her what she had meant when it was painfully obvious. Abilene had told him the truth of the situation. She had preempted what could have been a disaster.

Nadine is off limits, so don't bother.

CHAPTER NINE

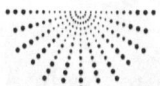

*W*hen Nadine saw that red-and-black Volkswagen camper van puff down the street toward her corner of the neighborhood, she freaked out five ways and dropped the hose she was holding. Water flowed all around her bare feet on the freshly cut grass.

She felt hot.

Sure, it was a hundred degrees in Savannah, and she should have watered the plants earlier in the morning, but having worked all night, she had overslept.

And now this.

The VW coasted to a stop right in front of her yard. It looked like the same 1962 van with a fresh coat of paint. Same old colors.

Dad bounced out and stretched.

Nadine prayed—begged!—for mercy.

If there was anyone in the whole wide world who could talk some sense into Mom, it would be Dad. Yet he was the last person Mom wanted to see. The fact that Dad was here now—by himself—could only mean one thing: he had failed to reconcile with Mom.

It would be up to Nadine again to bridge the gap, to be the messenger pigeon.

Here was the first half of the problem, crossing the lawn with his arms outstretched.

"Your favorite dad is here!" Dad shouted.

"You're my *only* dad." Nadine sloshed on the grass to greet him.

"Come here, sweetie!" Dad engulfed Nadine in a big bear hug. "It feels like I haven't seen you in years, Nadine."

Peeling away from Dad's sweat, Nadine smiled. "We had dinner two weeks ago, remember?"

Dad thought for a moment. "That's right. Your mom made fried chicken."

Nadine grinned. "The way you like it."

"Yep. She's the only one who can make butter-milk fried chicken just right..." His voice trailed off.

Nadine patted Dad's big arm. "We'll get her back. She just needs space."

"We got space! I told her we could go on a road

trip to the wide-open prairies." His shoulders sagged. "She said it's Cancun or nothing."

"So go to Cancun. What's the fuss?"

"We've already been to Cancun twice."

"Go again, if it makes Mom happy."

"Well, she'll be happy on the open road."

"She said that?"

"I said that."

"You're thinking for her again."

"I'm not." Dad pointed to his VW. "I put in a rebuilt engine just for her. I wanted to sell it, but she said we can't. Nostalgia, and all that."

"You spent your honeymoon in that van."

"Four weeks of bliss. She's the one who said we're going back on the road someday."

"Do both."

"What?" Dad knitted his bushy eyebrows together.

"Go on a road trip and go to Cancun."

"Can't do that, dear. Cancun is south. Colorado is west."

"I didn't say at the same time. Both of you are retired. Surely you have time for two trips." Nadine paused. "If you need money..."

"No need. She kept saying, 'Cancun or nothing.' Like she had to have her way, you know." Dad spread his chubby hands. "I said I got nothing. That's when the meat sauce burned."

"Your dinner."

"And it went downhill from there." Dad straightened up. "I love your mom and I want her back, but I'm not sure if it's going to happen. Your childhood home is on the market now. All my stuff is in storage because the real estate agent wants the yard cleared, not that we had any grass to begin with."

"Potential buyers like things uncluttered," Nadine explained. "My friend, Sabine, who sells million-dollar homes on Tybee Island, told me that the less junk—I mean, stuff—you have lying around, the more spacious it looks."

"But I don't want to sell."

"That's understandable." Nadine picked up the hose again to finish watering her brownish bushes.

"Let me." Dad took the hose from her. He frowned at the bushes. "Those bushes are dead, Nadine. We don't need to be watering dead plants."

"I thought they might come back."

"Like your mom?"

Nadine flinched. "She's not dead."

"But she's gone."

"She just needs time to think." It was a guess, but it had to do.

"Think about what?"

"Life and such."

Dad chuckled. "She told you that? She needed space to think about life and such?"

"No. I summarized it from our conversation."

"Ah. She called you."

Nadine nodded. "Mom and I always talk. You know that."

"That's why I'm here," Dad declared. "You can help. What are we going to do to get Mom back?"

We? Uh-oh. "We go to God."

"You mean to your church?" Dad asked.

"God. We go to God Himself. We pray. Ask for His help."

"He's not going to listen to me. I can tell you that. No siree."

"God does listen."

"If He does, why did your mother leave me?" Dad turned off the faucet.

"That's Mom's decision. We can't project our flawed human actions as something God has done or would have done, nor can we put words in God's mouth or blame Him."

"Yeah. Okay. Maybe, but why didn't God stop her?"

Nadine shrugged. "God's ways are so much higher than our ways."

"You are wise, sweetie."

"God is wise. I'm just repeating what the Bible

says." Nadine coiled up the green hose and put it into a box by the side of the house.

"What does it say about love?" Dad asked.

"Love is patient. Love is kind. Among other things." What did she know about love? Sure, she had the love of God, but when the Bible said that a man was to love his wife as Christ loved the church, that marriage business was lost on her.

Here were her parents. Separated after forty years of marriage. How sad.

"Let's go inside. Have some lemonade." Nadine opened the front door for Dad. It jammed. She jiggled the knob.

"I'll get that for you," Dad said.

There was a sureness in his voice that hadn't been there when he talked about getting Mom back.

Nadine determined that she would do her best to help her parents reconcile with each other. Maybe they could have the happy ending she doubted she'd ever have.

Brute force opened the door, and they went inside to a wobbly, whirring ceiling fan.

Dad pointed.

Nadine sighed. "Yes, Dad. You can fix that too."

She led the way into the kitchen.

"How long are you in town?" she asked, pouring lemonade for both of them.

"Not sure. If you don't mind, I'd like to stay for a while. Regroup, maybe. Think about my life."

"You can stay as long as you want." Nadine meant it.

"I can pay rent."

"No. No rent."

"I've got to do something."

"Well, you can find me a replacement bush."

"I can mow your lawn and water your yard."

"Deal!" Nadine didn't care for lawn work. Too hot, too sweaty, and she always came indoors smelling like grime and Georgia soil.

Dad shook his head as tears splattered onto his old shirt.

Nadine hugged him.

"Boy, it's going to be a tough Thanksgiving," Dad finally said. "Your mom's roast turkey is the best in the world."

Nadine nodded.

"Maybe you can learn to cook, Nadine."

"Uh. No time. I have a business to run. I guess we'd better pray that God brings Mom home to us before Thanksgiving, huh?"

"Or I'll be staying with you awhile."

"Stay as long as you like, Dad."

Nadine didn't mind Dad living with her at all, but she had been thinking about getting a cat. That would now have to wait. Dad was allergic to cats.

Well, she'd just have to pet Abilene's cat instead.

Nadine wondered how Bradley was faring, not having his owner hold him. As long as Abilene's dad was handling the cat litter, Nadine needn't worry about that. Still, it was too bad that she didn't have to go to Abilene's house all week. She kind of enjoyed chatting with—

Banish the thought!

Dad would never approve of a bon vivant ladies' man like Dante.

CHAPTER TEN

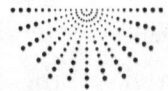

*D*ad had insisted on wearing his old Crocs to church. Yep, the ones with duct tape over a strap that had torn off. At least he had on clean clothes—his best pair of cargo shorts, and his best polo shirt that Nadine, thankfully, didn't have to iron.

They had been early because Dad hated to be late. He wanted to talk to Pastor Flores about Mom. Waiting for the service to start, and handing out programs with Abilene by her side, Nadine was mostly distracted by that very thing.

What on earth was Dad going to talk to Pastor Flores about? Mom just needed a bit of space and breathing room. Or something. That was all, right?

No need to make a big deal out of the separation.

No need to bring Pastor Flores into their private mess.

The whole situation bothered Nadine throughout the service and past the closing prayers. She had profusely asked God to forgive her for being so distracted that she couldn't remember what Pastor Flores had preached. She would have to listen to the sermon again this afternoon.

Thank God his sermons are online.

After church, Nadine was frantic when she couldn't find Dad. She didn't know how it had happened. She looked for him everywhere except the men's restrooms.

Flapping around, she ran into Abilene.

"Have you seen my dad?" Nadine asked.

"Calm down." Abilene smiled, stroking her belly. "He was talking to Pastor Flores, and they went downstairs."

"No."

"Don't worry about it. Sometimes they just need to talk. You know, mano a mano."

Nadine frowned. "I don't think that's the right phrase."

"What do you mean?"

"*Mano a mano* doesn't mean man to man, Abilene." Nadine's eyes darted toward the deck where the stairs went to the dining hall below. She wanted to run downstairs to get in on Dad's conversation, but something in her heart stopped her.

Was the Holy Spirit telling her something?

Abilene laughed. "Okay. Sorry. I did mean man to man, whatever the word is. Heart to heart. Point is, let them talk, Nadine. Your dad probably needs to air out some stuff. Want to go for lunch? Your dad's invited too."

"You guys better go ahead. Who knows how long their conversation is going to take."

"I'm sure that Pastor Flores and Heidi have lunch plans themselves. In fact, I'm surprised they even went downstairs. Usually Pastor Flores would schedule a meeting."

"And I used to schedule it for him until I got too busy with my own work." Nadine sighed.

That was an issue as well. Had she been so busy with Saylor Virtual Services that she had no time for ministry? No time to help out at church? No time to visit the elderly and pray for those in need? No time to even talk to people? Talk to—

Ah.

No time to talk with Mom and Dad.

Nadine recalled how she had told Mom on the phone that she couldn't talk more because she had work to do.

And Dad? Well, she had been plotting ways to keep him occupied while he was bunking at her

JAN THOMPSON

house. She had to think of how to get him busy so that she could get back to work.

It was always work, wasn't it?

What about family?

Nadine cringed at her own question.

"You all right?" Abilene asked.

When Nadine lifted up her heavy head, she saw Lars standing next to Abilene. He carried her Bible and purse for her. They were a cute couple. And baby made three. A nice family there.

Family.

That word again.

A conviction overcame Nadine's heart. God was trying to tell her something. Well, it seemed that He had been trying to tell her something for months. She hadn't been listening.

Family.

"I'm so tired, Abilene." Nadine was confessing more to God than to Abilene or to herself. "I've been working like a dog, and I'm plain old worn out."

"Uh-huh." Abilene pursed her lips.

Nadine knew what she was going to say.

I've been trying to tell you, Nadine.

"But if I don't work, I don't get paid." Justification. It didn't seem to work anymore. "Pray for me?"

"I will, Nadine. Always." Abilene hugged Nadine. "Lunch on me, okay?"

58

"No need." Out of the corner of her eyes, Nadine saw Dad. He didn't look happy.

"You go ahead," Nadine told Abilene. "We'll catch up with you."

Abilene got the message. She and Lars hurried off.

Dad stood right where Abilene had. "I'm not coming back to this church."

"I'm sorry. Something happened?"

"Everything happened. Your pastor"—Dad shook his head—"is some piece of work."

Nadine ushered Dad through the deck and down the ramp. "What did you talk to him about?"

"Your mom. And life in general."

"And what did Pastor Flores say?"

"He says I can't have a solution without faith, and salvation without Christ. What kind of church is this anyway?"

"Well, it's a Christian church, with members who believe in Christ for the salvation of their souls."

"Then I've come to the wrong church. I'm visiting someplace else next week."

Nadine tried to keep her cool. "It'll be hard to find a Christian church without Christ. A Christian church by definition is where Christians go to worship Christ."

"I'll go to a synagogue."

"It's a free country. Do what you want." Nadine and Dad crossed the road to where she had parked her car. "How about lunch with my friends?"

"Friends from your church?"

Nadine nodded. "We usually meet at Piper's Place after church on Sundays."

"Not today. I just want to go home." Dad got in the passenger side of Nadine's small car.

Home.

The word was not lost on Nadine.

"Then let's go home, Dad."

CHAPTER ELEVEN

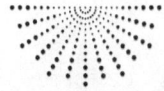

"*O*kay, Abilene. You win." Dante leaned back on the love seat. Across the coffee table, his sister was knitting.

Knitting!

Was this what Mom had called *nesting?*

Abilene rose from the recliner. "What did I win? Does it come with chocolate fudge?"

Normally, Dante would find that funny, but not today. Today, he had a problem. Two words: Nadine Saylor.

He wasn't sure when it had begun, but by the time he felt it, he couldn't stop thinking of her.

All morning, even when he had been brushing his teeth, he had thought of her. Puttering around the house wondering what to do in between checking emails, he had wondered whether he should have gone to church, after all, and sat next to Nadine.

I've got to get into her league.

Funny how it went. His Wharton MBA hadn't prepared him for Nadine.

"You win, Abilene. I'll stop dating." He meant it. "I'll go celibate."

"You're already celibate." Abilene's laughter filled the sunroom, rising to the whirring leaf-shaped fan on the ceiling and down again, slapping Dante's cheeks left and right and leaving a taste of shame in his mouth.

"You and I know that Grandma isn't going to put up with babies out of wedlock," Abilene added.

"But Nadine doesn't know that," Dante said. "She thinks I go through girlfriends."

"And whose fault is that?"

"You're not going to help me? What are siblings for?"

"Help you do what, Dante? Tell her you're free and clear?" Abilene stopped knitting. "Leave her alone. Nadine's better than this."

"Better? Who are you to judge?"

"I've known Nadine since college. I know more about her than you do."

"All I want to do is score a date with her. She's playing hard to get." Dante lifted his arms and crossed them behind his head. He closed his eyes and imagined Nadine sitting next to him right now on the love seat.

Just the two of them.

"Score? Listen to yourself, big Brother." Abilene frowned. "You know the best ladies are never easy to get. They're reserved for their future husbands alone. They save themselves for God's perfect spouse for them."

"And you're saying I fall short?"

Abilene almost nodded. Dante could see that slight jiggle in her curly hair. She stopped herself. Maybe it was for his sake.

"You skipped church this morning," Abilene said.

"Ah, an indictment. I slept in. It was too late for me to get going. I'm sure God understands."

"It's an easy thing—super easy—to go to church. We have room in the vehicle. All you had to do was get up, shower, eat some breakfast, and hop into the car. You couldn't do that."

"I was tired."

"The spirit is willing, but the body is weak."

Dante thought that Abilene was going to say more, but she had clammed up.

"I go to church, not as often as you do, but I don't miss Christmas and Easter. Ever. You know that." Dante massaged his thighs. He wished he could feel them. "If God wants me to go to church more—every Sunday, for example—then why doesn't He give me my legs back?"

"Give you? Your legs are not yours to keep. Do you remember the day we both got saved?"

"Yeah. At camp."

"High school seems so long ago, doesn't it?"

Dante nodded. Those were the days when he had never thought bad things could happen to him. He had lived wild and reckless, until God saved him that day at camp in the mountains. He had only gone to camp to meet the girls, but instead, he had met God, and He had changed his life.

Why did I start falling away from You?

He tapped his senseless knees. "This happened, Abilene. I'm a changed man since this happened to me."

"I'm sorry that your legs define who you are. The last time I checked, the Dante I know conquered the world, runs a multibillion dollar company—"

"Stop right there. You know as well as I do that Dad's still in charge. I'm the *future* CEO. The seat isn't warm." He chuckled. "Actually, I've been traveling so much with all these merger talks that I haven't been to my office in weeks. I don't know when Dad will let me take over Hot Dupree."

"When he sees consistent evidence of your maturity."

"He told you that?"

"I know Dad. I know how he thinks," Abilene said. "I also know how you think."

"You do, huh, little Sister? So tell me. How do I think?"

"You think that Nadine is a trophy and you must win her."

"Not just her. I want her heart. And I'm failing at this. I can't get one date with her. So help me out, Abilene."

"Then what?"

"What do you mean *what*?"

"After the date, what's next? What do you have in mind? Check her off your date list and move on to the next woman?"

Dante said nothing.

CHAPTER TWELVE

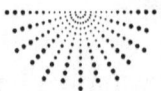

adine swung on the new wrought-iron swing as a hot breeze blasted her on the porch.

"What do you think?" Dad asked. "I oiled the hinges. No creaks."

"I like it," Nadine said softly.

"But?"

Nadine didn't respond. She curled her legs underneath her and waited for Dad to keep going. Knowing him, the less Nadine spoke, the more Dad would share his heart.

Right now, she needed to know what was going on between Dad and Mom. With Mom out there frolicking in Cancun with who knew who, the only person who knew the truth about her parents' marital strife was Dad.

Yeah, this dad who was busier salvaging junk than figuring out what went wrong with his marriage of forty years.

You can take the man out of the junkyard but you can't take the junk mentality out of—

Okay. Maybe that's too sarcastic.

"I'm going to get a few more," Dad went on. "Paint them in different colors. If I can make five hundred a month, I can help pay rent—"

"Dad."

"What?"

"Banish the thought. You're my dad. You stay here as long as you want. No rent, okay? Haven't I told you that?"

"I don't want to live off you."

"I lived off you most of my life, remember? Even through college, you were paying for me when I couldn't get a scholarship."

"You also worked, Nadine. You were the hardest working college student I knew."

"I'm the only college student you knew, Dad."

"Yeah. Most of your cousins flunked out." Dad nodded. "I'm glad your college is paid for and you don't have student loans following you around."

"God has been good to us."

Dad expelled some noise that startled Nadine. He got out of his chair and walked to the edge of the porch. "Don't bring God into this. He has nothing to do with us."

"No? I breathe. That's evidence that God exists. Life is not random chance and meaningless, haphazard hit-and-miss."

"Believe what you will."

"That's it, isn't it? Belief."

Belief had been what had led Nadine to Christ. She remembered the day she had lunch with Abilene on the campus of the Savannah College of Art and Design. They had been sophomores then, taking tough classes. Her entire life had changed that cool October day when she asked Jesus to save her. It had changed so radically that she had switched her major from fashion design to advertising. It had helped her now as a virtual assistant.

"Well, I believe that I should pay rent," Dad insisted.

"No. This house is paid off. I have no house payment. So I don't need your rent."

"Smart move to buy this house at foreclosure."

Nadine nodded. "God gave me that wisdom, Dad."

"I feel a lecture coming."

"No lecture. I'm only trying to tell you that God can give us wisdom as to how to get Mom back."

"If I get her back, then I'll believe in God."

"It doesn't work that way. The Bible says that we walk by faith, not by sight."

"That'd better be true, Nadine. I can't see your Mom coming back to me, is all I can say. She's gone. Gone." Dad blinked.

Nadine eased off the swing. Quickly, she bear-hugged Dad. "Don't worry. I've been praying, and I know God answers my prayers, and yours too, if you believe in Him."

"Does He answer my prayer if I don't believe in Him?" Dad asked.

"Never underestimate the power of God."

CHAPTER THIRTEEN

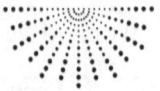

*D*ante wheeled into the nineteenth-century halls, the harlequin floors beneath his dress shoes, and antique Tiffany chandeliers above his combed hair. His heart wasn't into the glitter this evening, and he could think of a thousand places he'd rather be.

It felt weird being alone.

Sure, his security personnel was around somewhere, giving him berth and space, but ready to catch him if he slid off his wheelchair in some sort of embarrassing juxtaposition.

Ah, Waylon Diaz. Dante wasn't sure what he was going to do without him. Waylon had been working for him for some years now, traveling with him everywhere and fending off anyone who accosted him.

To be sure, Waylon wasn't his nurse, but he didn't need a nurse anymore. He was independent enough now, having settled into his life as a paraplegic.

Still, that expensive procedure coming up might help him walk again. He was scheduled to check into that Tokyo hospital soon.

Meanwhile, his independence had a limit. No worries. Dante knew that Waylon would take him out of this place and back to the safe haven of his sister's house if he felt sick.

Yeah, sick.

All afternoon, his stomach had been queasy. Might be something he had eaten.

No, I don't want to see a doctor.

A bevy of pretty ladies and handsome gentlemen greeted him. They all seemed to be around his age. The self-made millionaires, the old-money trust-fund babies, and everyone in between all wanted to say hello to the future CEO of the Hot Dupree empire.

Here came Jared Urquhart. Old money right there. Jared's family had been earning a fortune since the nineteenth century. This was his party place in Savannah.

"They made you look better than you do, man." Jared slapped Dante's shoulder. Hard.

Was it in spite or was it a friendly gesture?

"What are you talking about?" Dante asked.

"On the cover of *Money Sells Money* magazine."

"I know nothing about it." Yep. Since Chelsea quit, he was no longer in the know about anything!

"You made top ten most eligible billionaires in the world. Don't be coy."

The world?

Dante shrugged. Tried to remain cool. "Well, stuff like that comes and goes, Jared. I bet you're up there too."

"Nope. Apparently, I hit thirty-five and didn't make the cut. Oh, there she is. Someone I have to see. I'll talk with you later, man. Don't let the fame get to your head."

Don't worry. It can't.

I won't let it.

Or else Nadine will never go out with me.

Camera flashes blinded him as he blinked away the spotlight. Immediately, he knew if that ended up in the papers, he'd look terrible. He tried to keep his eyes open. Even smiled a bit for the media.

If Chelsea were here, she would have told him the news media were here following that *Money Sells Money* news. Without her, he would have to look it up on his own. Who had nominated him anyway?

Well, being the future CEO of Hot Dupree had put him in the hot seat.

That very thing he had craved all his adult life—to run Hot Dupree—now began to taste like ashes on his tongue.

Before he could find a way to get out of there, a woman whose assets were bursting out of a skintight red dress waltzed into his face and planted a wet kiss on his lips.

He couldn't back away. There were people all around him, people whose feet he would be running over with his wheelchair.

Waylon! Where's Waylon?

"Excuse me, ma'am," a deep voice said.

Waylon.

Thank God!

Dante nodded to his bodyguard as the latter pushed the wheelchair away from Miss Botox Lips.

"Thank you, Waylon." Dante had a hard time breathing. "Get me out of here."

"Thought you'd never ask."

"Find a way to get those photographs off the media."

"Impossible, sir. It's probably on the Internet as we speak."

"I should've known."

Only one more strike against him in Nadine's eyes.

CHAPTER FOURTEEN

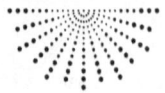

*N*adine was busy working on three twenty-seven-inch monitors in her bedroom when she heard a loud commotion coming from her front yard. She tried to keep working, but the noises increased. Beeping noises, grating noises, men shouting, wheels turning.

She slapped both palms on her old recycled oak desk.

It was probably Dad again.

The clock above her registered two minutes to noon.

"Two more minutes! That's all I'm asking, Dad!"

Nadine sprang out of her ergonomic chair. She was still in her pajamas—an old blouse and cotton gym shorts—and her hair was coiled and pinned into a chignon on top of her head.

She couldn't believe what she saw when she peeked out the front windows in the living room. She ran outside and felt the heat of the driveway beneath her thin rubber flip-flops. That was nothing compared to what was boiling in the rest of her now.

There was Dad, arms up, motioning for the giant truck to back up more.

"Dad!" Nadine called out.

"One sec!" Dad shouted back. "Stay back where it's safer, Nadine."

Safer? What is he talking about?

Nadine stepped back on the grass and nearly tripped over something hard. She looked down and gasped. Parts of wrought-iron fences and other rusty metalworks, broken and whole, were scattered all over her front lawn.

Oh no.

Oh no, oh no, oh no...

She clasped her palms to her mouth. "Lord Jesus, give me the words to say to stop this madness!"

Dad turned toward her. "Do we have lunch ready? I should be ready to eat in about ten minutes."

"What?"

"Lunch, Nadine. Lunch!"

She had heard Dad the first time. But the dichotomy was giving her a headache. Dad staying with her temporarily was one thing, but nothing in their agreement had said anything about turning her house into a junkyard!

She watched in fear as the giant green dumpster was lowered onto her driveway. It was at least seven feet tall, and metal pieces were jutting out of it here, there, and everywhere.

Nadine stood there, stunned. This was looking more and more like her childhood home, a veritable junkyard of other people's trash. Nadine wondered if Dad would ever outgrow it.

"Dad?" She finally bleated out the words.

"What, my sweet daughter?" Dad placed both arms on his waist. "Isn't she a beauty? I can just imagine the amazing things I can make out of all that. Only five hundred dollars for everything. A steal."

He laughed. "Get it? Steal? Steel?"

Nadine wasn't laughing. At. All.

What were the neighbors going to think? Say? Complain about? Sure, this area wasn't uppity enough for any homeowner's associations to pin notices to her mailbox, but she had tried to keep the yard nice and clean.

Nice and clean.

Not this.

Nadine could see it now. This entire place—her paid-for property—would turn into Dad's old house, the one he was selling.

"What are you going to do with all that?" Nadine asked, praying at the same time that God would give her grace to handle Dad.

Maybe this was his therapy. The separation from Mom seemed traumatic for him. He had never been away from her in their entire marriage. And now Dad had to adjust to his new normal. If Mom never returned to him, he'd have to go at it alone.

Yeah, surrounded by junk.

Nadine prayed for understanding. Still, she had to draw a line. This was her house. Her house, not Dad's. She had paid it off and owned it free and clear. Sure, it was little, and only had two bedrooms. But it was her house.

And as the lady of the house, she had the right to make the house rules.

But Dad...

Poor Dad...

"Dad?" Nadine said carefully.

"Yes?"

"What are you going to do with all this trash —treasure?"

"I'll make some garden artwork."

"Artwork?"

Dad nodded.

"And?" Nadine waited.

"And sell them."

"To whom?"

"To your neighbors, art collectors in Savannah and beyond, art appreciators, anybody."

Anybody? "We need to talk."

"Over lunch." He motioned for Nadine to get going. "I'll be inside in just a few minutes. I have a surprise for you."

"A surprise?" No more! Nadine wasn't sure she could handle it.

"Go inside. Don't want you to spoil it by seeing it first."

"Now I'm curious."

But Dad said no more. He left her wondering as he went to talk to the truck driver.

Nadine stepped back into her house on wobbly knees. She glanced this way and that and spotted a neighbor standing at the fence, waving to her with one hand while holding his pipe with the other.

She waved back, putting on her best fake smile.

CHAPTER FIFTEEN

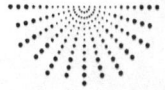

"*D*ad, which is more important to you: Mom or your junk?" Nadine rummaged through the pantry for two paper plates. For some reason she almost took out three paper plates, as if Mom were here.

Nadine noticed that Dad didn't protest her using the word *junk*.

"Do I have to choose?" Dad said at the small breakfast nook-cum-dining table as he cut the chocolate cake—the surprise.

"Be serious. Your marriage is at stake."

"I'm always serious."

"About Mom?" Nadine sat down by a wall of windows leading to the covered porch outside. It was this wall that had sold her the tiny house. Sabine had shown her this property one sunny afternoon several years prior, and when Nadine saw the sunshine on the hardwood floor, she knew this place was where she wanted to live.

Well, until the August heat wave came.

Year after year.

There it was again, that August sun, beating down on her poor, dry yard, badly in need of watering again.

"About Soledad. About you. I've always been very serious about the two most important people in my life." Dad sat down to dig into his piece of cake.

"How come your piece is bigger than mine?" Nadine asked, keeping an eye on her iPad, which she had placed on the table.

Anytime now, Epstein and Waddell would text her to ask for one more thing. For all the income those two speakers brought in per annum, they were some of the most disorganized speakers she had ever met.

"Coz I'm Papa!" Dad roared.

If Mom were here, she'd be laughing at that roar, which she had said Dad had been practicing since their wedding day.

Forty-one years next spring.

Why did it all have to end?

"Like the cake?" Dad asked, oblivious to the thoughts in Nadine's mind.

"It's yummy good. A tad too sweet, but just the way you like it, right?"

Somewhere in the process of hauling iron scraps from yard sales and junkyards around Savannah, Dad had managed to stop at Publix to buy her a chocolate cake.

"Thank you for the cake, Dad."

"Don't mention it. And wait until you see what I'm going to do with the scrap metal outside."

Nadine tried to keep her cool.

"About your question, yes, I'm making some yard ornaments for your mom. This is why I bought the pieces. I'm going crazy thinking about her, and this is how I'm getting out my frustrations."

Whoa. Okay.

Poor Dad.

"Soledad has always been—and still is—the love of my life." Dad's voice crumbled. The self-assured artist who had always given Nadine what she wanted was now at the end of his rope. He had lost his one true love.

One true love?

Nadine couldn't believe what had percolated through her mind.

One true love was the stuff of fairy tales, not real life.

This was real life, where love was messy and untidy and difficult to sustain without God's help.

Still, it was up to Dad whether or not he wanted God to solve his problems.

"So you think that making garden sculptures will bring Mom back," Nadine said.

Dad tilted his head. "You don't believe me?"

"All I know is that I'm praying for God's perfect will for you and Mom. I pray that both of you would get back together again. You two need each other."

"I don't know, Nadine. I think I need her more than she needs me."

"What do you mean?" Nadine didn't dare guess where Dad was heading with that statement.

"If she needs me, she wouldn't have left."

"That so? I'd like to think your love for each other is deeper than that."

"You think she still loves me?"

"We'll have to find out." Nadine wondered about that herself.

"How?"

"We go see Mom in Cancun."

Dad chortled. "Seriously?"

Nadine nodded. "Is your passport current?"

"Only because your mom made me renew it. Like I was going out of the country anytime soon."

"Therein is your problem. You're not on the same page as Mom."

Dad stared at her.

"What?" Nadine finished her chocolate cake.

She wondered if she should have a second piece, then decided against it.

"I'm sorry, Nadine. So sorry." Dad put down his fork on his empty plate.

"For what?"

"For making you go to art school at SCAD."

"I liked SCAD." The Savannah College of Art and Design had been good for her.

"Art school is my thing, not yours."

"I do art too."

"When was the last time you did anything artsy?"

"Well..." Nadine couldn't remember.

"Exactly."

"I've been busy with my VA work."

"Right. You're good at this. You're very organized. You can take someone's messy calendar and schedule it into order. You can see a situation and assess, evaluate, advise. I should never have tried to push you into art. You clearly have your mom's business acumen."

"Thank you for the compliment, but God worked it all out for my good. I was saved in college, remember?"

"I do. And I'd thought you had joined a cult."

"Yeah. Mom thought the same thing too."

"Until she got saved as well. And now it's the two of you against me."

"We're not against you. We love you."

Dad didn't seem to believe her. "Look where love has left me. Alone without your mom."

"You should go get her back." Nadine checked her iPad. One round-trip plane ticket to Cancun at the peak of summer would cost...

Yikes. "We'll have to wait until I get paid. I don't see how I can buy you a ticket until September."

"I have money—oh wait. I, uh..."

"Let me guess. You just spent most of it, if not all, on the junk in the front yard."

"Art, not junk. When we sell the house..." Dad paused. "By then, she might have a new boyfriend."

"You mean Mom?"

"Yes. She's so beautiful that every man would want her."

"But she only loves you."

"That remains to be seen."

Nadine didn't argue with Dad. It was pointless.

Clearly Dad was heartbroken, disappointed, and perhaps slightly miffed that Mom had left him.

The sooner they remedied this, the better.

They?

Sorry, Lord. You. You are the only One who can fix a marriage.

CHAPTER SIXTEEN

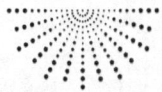

"*T*hanks for coming on such a short notice." Dante's voice was thick. He pointed to his security guy nearby. "Waylon here says he doesn't change cat litter."

The security guard's face didn't twitch. "It's above my pay grade."

"No problem. I'd be happy to do it." Nadine stepped into the sitting room just inside the terrace. She closed the door behind her. "No charge."

Dante pointed to her. "See that, Waylon? Generosity at work."

"Whatever you say, sir." Waylon cleaned up his table space.

Nadine figured he was probably on break. It didn't matter either way.

She was here, and she'd take care of Bradley.

It had taken her two hours to get here after Dante had texted her to say that his dad had to leave town due to some issues at the factory outside Baton Rouge, and would she kindly come over to deal with Bradley's litter box?

"Lunch is at noon," Dante reminded Waylon. "Piper's Place. On me."

"Thank you, sir. I'll go on break now."

"You do that." Dante coughed.

"You okay? You sound stuffed up." She wasn't sure if she wanted to get near Dante. The last thing she needed right now was to catch anything. She had too much work to do to be sick.

"Just a cold. Mostly in my head and chest. That's all."

"That's all? You poor thing. Have some chicken soup."

"I did."

"Who cooked it for you?"

"Campbell."

"Canned?" Nadine raised her eyebrows.

"Better than nothing. It's pretty good."

"I'll bring you some homemade soup tonight."

Dante looked at her in a funny way. "For me? I'm trying not to read too much into that."

"I see your wit isn't sick."

"Sorry. Yes, I'd love some homemade soup, but you don't have to. I don't want to impose."

"Nothing to it. I'll cook enough for my dad and me, and I'll bring some in a slow cooker."

Dante sneezed into a wad of tissue paper. He reached for more, but the box hanging off his wheelchair armrest was empty.

Nadine looked around for another box. She spotted one on the coffee table. She brought it to Dante.

"Thanks." Dante blew his nose.

"Are you taking anything for that?" Nadine asked.

"Some cold meds Waylon got me from the pharmacy."

Nadine tried not to check her watch, but seriously, she had to get back to work—

Ministry.

Yes, that.

She had enough time—plenty of time—to finish all those social media updates she had to do for Jurgen and Waddell. Oh yes, and Epstein too.

This morning, she was here for such a time as this. Perhaps God had a reason for this.

"Where's Bradley?" Nadine asked.

"Somewhere."

"Okay. I'll go change his litter. Do you need anything else from me?"

Dante's pause was so long Nadine started to worry that she had said something that could be misconstrued. "I meant if there's anything I can do for you while I'm here, while nobody else is around. Oh, that also came out kind of wrong."

"Waylon is here. We're not alone," Dante explained.

"Good. I don't want people to talk."

"About us?" Dante groaned. "You saw the pictures from last night's gala."

"They're all over Twitter. Dante Dupree has a new squeeze."

Dante laughed and coughed at the same time. "I think her dress is three or four sizes too small."

"I wasn't talking about her dress."

"No?"

"No. I was talking about the kiss. It looked good on camera, like you do it all the time."

Dante's eyes met hers. "And that bothers you?"

"What? No." Nadine stepped back. "It can't bother me."

"Because?"

"We're not—there's nothing going on between us."

"I wish there were."

"It can't happen, Dante." Nadine backed away. "Okay, let me change the litter, and then I have to get back to work—"

"Nadine."

"Lots of clients waiting for me to solve their problems today—"

"Nadine."

"I'll come back this afternoon with your chicken soup—"

"Nadine."

"Stop calling my name." She was standing at the door to the laundry room, some fifteen feet away from Dante. Her fingers gripped the handle to the glass-paneled door. For a split second, she thought the door itself shook in her hand, but maybe it was just her imagination.

Why would she be nervous?

It was only Dante.

Faraway Dante.

CHAPTER SEVENTEEN

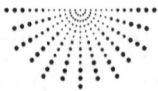

*D*ante wheeled closer to where Nadine was standing in front of the laundry room.

She wanted to cry. For no reason, she wanted to cry.

Dante stopped a couple of feet away from her.

"When was the last time you let anyone get close to you?" Dante asked.

"Not anyone who has a cold, for sure." She had learned it from Dad. When times got tough, find light moments. Turn the tables.

Or failing that, focus on something else.

"Be serious."

"None of your business, Dante."

"It is now."

"Why is that?"

"I care, Nadine."

"What for?"

"Can't you tell?" Dante sneezed again.

"I can tell, all right, that you are a sick puppy. I'll bring the chicken soup as soon as I can. Meanwhile, you need to get to bed and get some sleep."

"Yes, Dr. Saylor."

Before Nadine could say anything more, Bradley appeared, going toward his litter box.

"I guess we'll wait a bit for him to be done." Nadine sighed. "Do you want me to make you some hot tea or something? Have you eaten your breakfast?"

"I had cereal. Abilene made some for me before she left for work. Selena should be here shortly with my lunch."

Nadine should have expected that. Selena was Abilene's personal chef. Lars had insisted that Abilene not mess around with greasy pots and pans and hot stovetops while she was pregnant. She was very pampered.

"You're on your own today?" Nadine asked.

"I'm working, actually."

"You're sick. You should rest."

"I don't have a choice. My assistant quit on Saturday, and I'm on my own until I find someone to replace her." Dante blew his nose.

"I'm sorry."

"I can't run this company without her. She does all my scheduling."

Bradley strutted away without as much as a by-your-leave. Nadine shook her head. "They say cats don't have owners, only staffers. I can see that."

"You have your own cat?" Dante asked, as if he wanted to keep talking to prevent Nadine from leaving.

"Not yet. I wanted to get one, but Dad has just moved in with me, and he's allergic to cats. I'm going to have to wait until he goes home."

"I'm sorry."

"Me too. It's stupid how my parents fight all the time—oh, sorry. TMI."

"Say no more. None of my business that your parents are sort of like other normal couples."

Nadine smiled. "Well, Mr. Wit, I'd like to stay here and chat, but I have a business to run, poop to scoop, and clients to solve problems for."

Dante nodded as he reversed his wheelchair. "Say, if a new company wants to hire you, how do they contact you?"

"I'm not taking any new clients at this time, so the contact button on my website is disabled." Nadine found the litter bag on a wire shelf above the washing machine.

"It's only temporary. Maybe two or three weeks

until Phil—my manager—interviews Chelsea's replacement."

"What did she do?" Nadine listened as Dante listed all the things that sounded like what a virtual assistant did, what she had been doing for the previous six or seven years for her clients: scheduling their activities, answering their emails, establishing contacts, being at their every beck and call.

"I have a merger meeting tomorrow," Dante continued. "Dad's going to fly in directly to the meeting. As you can tell, I'm not a hundred percent. I just need someone to remind me if I missed anything."

"I can't be up to speed in one day, Dante. Besides, I have nine clients asking stuff from me, and two of them are very demanding. I have to fix their problems today, or I lose their business."

Dante nodded. "Okay. When are you available to take on a new client?"

"Available? Probably never."

"Even if I pay you twice what they pay you?"

Nadine breathed in deeply. "That's not it, Dante. I just don't have enough time of day. I get very little sleep at night—sometimes just three hours —in order to get all my work done."

"If you had more income, you could hire a minion to do some of the lesser work for you. All that social media stuff, for example." Dante waved his hands. "You can focus on your high-paying clients while your part-time employees—maybe college kids who need part-time work—do the menial busywork for you."

"Hmmm. That's a good idea. I do hire a college kid to fill in for me when I'm overbooked or out of town."

"I'm not the future CEO of Hot Dupree for nothing. I earned it, you know."

"And here I was, thinking Grandma Dupree is giving the company to you because you're cute."

Dante's eyes brightened. "You think I'm cute?"

"I retract my statement."

"Too late. I heard you when you said it."

"I unsaid it."

"You can't *unsay* it!" Dante coughed.

He wheeled toward a side table near an armchair and reached for a bottled water. He leaned too far forward and started to topple.

"Dante!" Nadine sprinted toward him, arms outstretched. She reached him in no time and pushed his chest back against the wheelchair seat.

Dante looked more embarrassed than ever. "Ah, I guess I forgot my torso belt."

Without a word, Nadine picked up the plastic bottle and handed it to him.

Her heart still beat a mile a minute, and she couldn't believe how horrified she had felt when she thought he was going to fall over. She knew that he was paralyzed from the waist down, and there was no way he could have stopped the fall, with the wheelchair wheels not being locked in place.

She breathed in slowly, trying to get calm again.

She felt warm fingers on her wrist. They were Dante's.

She wasn't as germaphobic as she used to be, but that hand probably needed to be washed. Yet instead of feeling repulsed, Nadine felt compassion for this man who could have been seriously injured had he fallen off his wheelchair and hit his head on the hard slate floor.

Something drew her to Dante.

I hope it isn't pity.

He's not a man to be pitied.

Maybe it was compassion for a fellow human being. Compassion? Was that all?

Nadine just stood there, letting Dante's hand remain on her wrist.

He said nothing more to her.

And she said nothing more to him.

CHAPTER EIGHTEEN

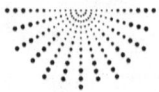

*S*he made me chicken soup.
　　　She went home and made me chicken soup.

Dante didn't know how to process that. His synapses were firing all at once. He was seeing stars. That, plus a sinus headache just made for a very confusing minute.

He had taken a long nap after lunch. It was almost six o'clock now, and yes, he was hungry. Perhaps that hunger had made him think too much about the chicken soup.

It's only soup!

He stared at her.

"Well?" Across the table, Nadine clasped her hands together, her pretty fingers interlocking. That rose fingernail polish looked feminine.

Very feminine.

"You don't like it?" Nadine asked slowly.

"No, no. I mean, yes, I like it. I do."

"But?"

Dante stirred the soup with the spoon. "Nobody outside my family has cared for me like this."

Nadine waved her pretty nails in the air. "Oh, don't read too much into it. I've made chicken soup for Abilene before. I do it for all my friends when they're sick."

"So you consider me a friend?" Dante wiped his lips with the cloth napkin. *What a lovely thought, that.*

"You're my friend's brother."

"Is that all I am?" He tried not to show his disappointment.

"Did you expect more?"

"I suppose not."

Nadine stood up. She went looking for her purse nearby. "Enjoy your soup. I have to get back to my dad. He's in the doldrums."

"I heard."

"Of what?"

"Your mom left your dad."

Nadine's shoulders sagged. "Abilene told you."

"Yes, but only because we were praying."

"It's not public knowledge, and I'd rather you don't talk about it." Nadine's voice hardened.

"We're trying to solve the problem, and I'd like to keep it in the family. I'm sorry Abilene told you."

Dante felt that he had hit a nerve. "My sister told me in confidence. Don't blame her. We were sitting around, talking, and she was very concerned for your family. It just came out, really."

Nadine nodded. "My parents love each other very much. They've been married for forty years. They had an argument. Mom burned dinner. Dad got mad. And she walked out."

"Forty years. I guess they're a few years ahead of my parents." Dante looked up. "Very few couples stay married that long anymore."

Nadine sniffed. "I know. If I were to marry, it would be for life."

"Good for you, Nadine. Unfortunately, for me, it'll be a short life."

Nadine looked horrified. "What do you mean?"

Dante felt bad. He didn't mean to scare her. "Nothing for you to worry about. A paraplegic's life expectancy is less than that for a normal person."

"Like how much less?" Nadine picked up her purse from the oversized armchair nearby. She produced an iPad from the giant bag.

Dante shrugged. Tried to play cool as he waited for the house Wi-Fi to kick in on Nadine's iPad.

"Twenty-some percent. That's not bad." Nadine

scrolled on her browser. "Besides, God has our lives in His hands. Why are you telling me about death?"

"I don't know. We were talking about our parents' long marriages."

"Isn't that interesting?" Nadine smiled once more. "Both of our parents have long marriages."

"So there's hope yet for our generation?"

"Ha. Maybe." Nadine slung her purse over her shoulder. "I'll see you around. Tomorrow morning, I guess."

"Dad's flying in at noon, so he could deal with Bradley's litter later in the day." Dante wheeled around the table.

"You don't have to see me to the door."

Dante wheeled back to his soup.

"Why don't I come in the morning? That way your dad doesn't have to worry about Bradley."

"Trust me. Dad's not worried about Bradley. We've got bigger problems tomorrow."

Nadine stopped. "Something you'd like me to pray for? Or not. I don't care. I'm not inquisitive."

"Merger talks tomorrow with Coastal Condiments. Something doesn't feel right, but I can't put my finger on it. The last thing we need is to go with my gut, you know, since I can't even feel my gut sometimes." Dante laughed.

Nadine did not laugh at all.

Dante cleared his throat. "I'm the one who

should be worried. I lost Chelsea, and she's my right hand and both legs."

"I thought you have replacements being interviewed."

"For later." Dante lifted the entire bowl to his lips and drank the chicken soup. "This is really good. I feel my sinuses clearing now. We should market this."

Nadine wasn't amused. "Don't you have other assistants you can call on?"

"Huh? Oh. Well, not anyone I can trust. They all work for Phil. I've been talking to Ming, and the way it's going, I might have to let Phil go."

He wasn't going into details, but Ming Wei, the private investigator friend of Abilene's, had uncovered some hanky-panky stuff on Phil's online activities. Ming was still digging, but Dante didn't like what he had uncovered thus far.

All this undermining of Dante's leadership at Hot Dupree didn't sit well with Dante.

At all.

"When is your new assistant supposed to be at her desk?" Nadine asked.

"I'm hoping next week."

"So you're on your own this week?"

"In a way, yes, but Dad has a team I'm hitch-hiking on."

"So you're not suffering."

"It would be good to have someone to watch my back," Dante said slowly. He wasn't sure how to broach the subject. Nadine had already turned him down once. "How much do you charge per hour as a VA?"

"A hundred per hour in an emergency."

"Seriously?"

"No, Dante. I charge way less than that, but since I don't want to work for you, and I see where this conversation is headed, I just did some multiplications in my head. It's to throw you off. Did I succeed?"

"I'll pay you two hundred dollars an hour to sit with me through the merger talks. Two hours, maybe three, tops."

Nadine stood rooted where she was. "Seriously?"

"And you'd still cost me less than what my corporate attorney charges by the hour."

"Well...I could use the money. I am raising funds to fly Dad to Cancun to rescue Mom from herself."

Dante smiled. Ah, his power of persuasion was still sharp. "Tell you what. I'll send him to Cancun free of charge on my Gulfstream."

Nadine's eyes widened, and her jaw dropped. "You. Are. Kidding."

It was a sight to see. Dante knew he had her.

"All I ask is that you sit with me at the meeting and listen for something I might miss. Abilene says you have sharp ears."

Nadine frowned.

"She meant it as a compliment."

"Oh."

"I'll pay you by the hour," Dante added.

"What are you looking for? Do you know what I do?"

"You're a VA, aren't you? That's an administrative assistant? That's what Chelsea did for me."

"Yes, but..."

"Be a fly on the wall. What do you say? Can you start right now? Hey, I have an idea. If your dad is packed and ready to go, my pilot can fly him to Cancun tomorrow afternoon."

"Tomorrow?" Nadine gasped. *Praise the Lord that Dad's passport is current.* "Dad can go find Mom tomorrow?"

"You can go too, if you like—after the meeting. In fact, we can all go. My G650 can seat eight people." He knew that Nadine didn't fly well, but he still offered it. The most she could do was to turn him down.

"I don't fly if I can help it, but Dad can go," she said. "Besides, I have to work. You serious about this?"

"Yep. Thing is, my meeting is at two tomorrow afternoon. We need to get you up to speed pronto."

"Two o'clock?" The clock on the wall said there were fewer than twenty-four hours for her to "get up to speed." Besides, she had her own clients—

Dad goes to Cancun to get Mom back.

"Okay, I'll do it." Nadine dug for her iPad again. "I'll have to reschedule a few things. A lot of things. And I can't work between six and nine tonight."

"Oh? You have a date?"

"I have church. We have Wednesday night Bible study."

Dante remembered now that Abilene had mentioned Riverside Chapel activities. He felt sorry that he had been slack. He should ask God to forgive him, but then...

"Would you like to come to church with me tonight, considering you skipped church Sunday?" Nadine asked. "We're studying Galatians, if you're interested."

Dante wasn't sure what to say. Nadine had just invited him to church.

He shouldn't read too much into it. But she had forgotten something, hadn't she? "I have a cold, as you know."

Nadine gasped. "I don't know what I was thinking."

"I did miss church. I slept in Sunday morning," Dante confessed.

"Normally, if you missed church Sunday morning, you'd try to go on Sunday night, or at the very least, Wednesday night. Made up for it."

"Could one ever make up for missing church?"

"Not really, but God knows what's going on."

God knows what's going on.

"I don't know why I was too lazy to go to church Sunday, and honestly, I wasn't sick then. I didn't feel sick until Monday night or Tuesday morning."

"So you could've gone to church Sunday night."

"Yeah, but I have to say Riverside is not my church. It's Abilene's church. It's your church. I always go when I'm at home. But when I'm out of town or out of the country, it just isn't convenient."

"I don't know, Dante. Convenience versus Christ. Take your pick."

Dante wheeled back. "You know, I don't know if I want to be scolded."

"I'm not—sorry. It's not my place. It's God's business to convict, not mine. Please accept my apologies. I'm not usually this pushy."

"No, no. You spoke the truth. I was too lazy to go to church on Sunday. That's the honest truth."

Silently, Dante asked God to forgive him for sleeping in Sunday morning instead of making it to church. He wasn't on vacation, after all. Then again, even on vacations, there was no taking time off from worshipping God, was there?

"I'll go to church with you tonight," Dante said.

"You can't now. You're sick. You'll make everybody sick."

"You're confusing, Nadine. You invited me to church tonight."

"I told you that I didn't know what overcame me."

"Right. So I have an excuse right now for missing church tonight."

"I'm sure God can see you're really sick."

Dante waited for Nadine to say more. She took a while.

"Okay," she finally said. "We have maybe two hours of work before I have to leave. Give me five minutes to email you a contract, and then we can get started."

"I like that. Very good." Dante appreciated Nadine's no-nonsense approach. A contract eliminated ambiguities in their agreement.

"While you're prepping your contract, I'll go get my laptop," Dante said. "Everything you need is in there. Chelsea has—had—full access to it."

Nadine looked alarmed. "You let her access your personal laptop?"

"Yes. Why not?" Dante headed for his bedroom.

"So... After putting all this knowledge about

Hot Dupree into her head, she has now resigned and carried off all that data to her next place of employment."

"I'm not worried, Nadine. People come and go. Besides, she signed a nondisclosure agreement."

"Is an NDA enough to stop her from sharing your company secrets with her new employer, whoever it might be?"

Dante thought about it. "I guess, for some people, nothing is ever enough."

CHAPTER NINETEEN

$\mathscr{T}$here had to be a reason behind the austere decor of this renovated 1930s office building on Drayton Street. Nadine surveyed the severe furnishings in the Coastal Condiments conference room, where all the black-and-white seats looked like molded plastic out of a B-rated 1950s movie and where the walls were covered with flat screens instead of real windows to the outside.

Something about the whole setup smelled fishy.

Well, yes, Coastal Condiments also specialized in fish sauce for its largely Southeast Asian clientele on the other side of the world. But that was beside the point.

Prior to the meeting, Nadine had called Sabine Hu-Wei to get more information about this Coastal Condiments' property. Quite a find, it was.

This was a seventy-thousand-square-foot building appraised at fifteen million dollars.

Surely Coastal Condiments could afford to hire better interior designers.

Nadine tapped her pen on her crossed-over legs as she listened to the negotiators and their CEOs playing ping-pong with their companies, as if stocks were nothing but round balls to be tossed about.

They were hunched over a large table made of some sort of recycled product. It was an artistic table molded to look like burled walnut, but was impervious to coffee, as she had found out when Dante had spilled some of that stuff on his side of the table when they had first arrived.

Masterfully, his fast fingers had rescued the mug, etched with the Coastal Condiment logo, but not before some of the Kona had splashed out.

Nadine had sprung up, grabbed a stash of napkins from a coffee cart nearby, and cleaned up the mess before Dante could say *thank you*, which he had done with his eyes.

"Would you like fresh coffee, sir?" Nadine remembered asking Dante.

"No, thanks, Nadine." He had said it loudly, as she recalled.

And that was how the other party knew her name.

For two hours, Nadine had been avoiding the

stares of one of the Coastal Condiments employees—or one she had assumed was an employee.

She stopped tapping her pen and looked up.

Sure enough. He was glancing her way again.

What's up?

When the CEOs decided to take a thirty-minute break, Devon Dupree, Dante's dad, continued to speak with Dante as everyone else started filing out.

Nadine wanted some fresh air herself, but first, she wanted to see if Dante needed anything from her. Unfortunately, someone stopped her.

"Hi. Nadine, right?"

Nadine prayed for mercy. "Yes. And you are?"

"Brock Tennyson." His outstretched hand asked to be shaken.

Nadine shook it confidently. He had smooth hands. Very smooth. And nicely manicured. She wondered how he had time for such grooming.

"Would you like a snack? A drink? Some tea?"

It was four o'clock. But. "Water would be fine."

"Let's get some in the break room."

When Nadine hesitated, he smiled. "Lots of people there."

"Sure." Nadine bagged her pen and notepad. She picked up her bag.

"Are you electronics adverse?" Brock asked.

"Because you see me using a notepad instead of my iPad?"

"I got it. You don't want your boss to see you doodling on the job."

Nadine smiled. Far from it. She had a spiral-bound notepad instead of her usual iPad because she was trying to concentrate on the meeting instead of thinking of the million-and-one things she had to do for all her other clients.

She had taken this short gig because it afforded Dad a free flight to Cancun. He was on his way now. Nadine's friend, Ming Wei, had asked around and found out where Mom had been staying for the past week.

Thank God for private investigator friends.

"Tell you a secret." Brock lowered his voice. "I've been doodling too."

"You have?" Nadine wondered what he was up to.

"Yeah. It's a done deal. That meeting is just cosmetic."

"You don't say."

"Uh-huh. You looked bored back there. Want to come work for me?"

"Bored? I looked bored? Was it my makeup?" Or lack thereof?

"You come across as smart and intelligent. So why are you working for Hot Dupree?"

"I like the benefits."

"When did you start work?"

"This week." *Okay, yesterday.*

"Is there a probation period?"

What is he up to? "What do you mean?"

"Two months there, and you quit?" Brock ushered her past the water cooler to a drab break room with more cheap chairs. "Come work for me. They all do."

"They all who?"

"I'll see that you get paid three times whatever they're paying you."

"Triple my salary? Wow. Can you do that?"

"Yes. I pull strings. Nothing to it." Brock shrugged. "Pay off your car, your mortgage. Take a vacation. Lots of things you can do with more pay."

"You're assuming I'm not paid enough."

Brock pointed to her chunky pumps. "Old shoes. You need a wardrobe update."

Ha. Old shoes? I don't care. These are my favorite pumps! I wear them anywhere.

"You're a confident man." Nadine realized what she had said. Well, perhaps he was, in more ways than one.

"Sure am. Tell you another secret?" Brock leaned toward Nadine. He smelled wonderful.

Nadine held her breath.

"You won't be the first to cross over our fence this year."

Not the first? Who else had left Hot Dupree this year?

This man is brazen. Cocky.

"You're very persuasive," Nadine said.

Brock shrugged. "Tea? Coffee?"

Has he already forgotten that I asked for water?

"Water will do." Nadine tried not to react when Brock's fingers brushed hers as he handed her the cold bottle of water.

Lord, forgive me, but I have to go fishing.

"You were pretty good back there in the conference room," Nadine began.

"Yep."

"Like you were born to lead." Buttering him up with the truth, Nadine didn't disclose whom she thought he might lead.

"Sure."

"What exactly do you do for Coastal Condiments?"

"I work in the office of the VP of marketing."

"Marketing? Nice. You sound like you could sell me anything." Nadine wondered if Dante would keep him on the payroll if Hot Dupree bought Coastal Condiments. "What's in the merger for you? A new office? Top level, maybe?"

The edge of his lips curled. "Come work for me and I'll tell you."

"Work for you? You mean for the new Coastal Condiments?"

He nodded. "We're meant for greater things."

What is he saying? Once the negotiations went through, Coastal Condiments would be a subsidiary of Hot Dupree, right?

For all practical purposes, Brock Whatshisname would lose his job.

All Nadine had to do was tell Dante about this conversation, and it was over for him.

Unless...

Brock must have been watching her eye movements. "You like my tie?"

He lifted it up for her to see. Under the break room ceiling light, Nadine spotted his watch.

No way. A knockoff leather-strapped Patek Philippe? Or the real thing?

Nadine's eyes flitted to the pattern on his tie. He was waving it about.

"Intricate," she said.

"Yep."

It was an expensive-looking silk tie. Nadine wondered whether to disclose that she had studied fashion at SCAD—before she had switched to marketing—and could tell that his tie was at least a hundred dollars, maybe more, but she thought better of it.

The less Brock knew about her, the less cautious he would be.

"A gift from your girlfriend, perhaps?" she asked instead.

Brock laughed. "No, no. My girlfriend and I broke up. I'm on the market."

Market? Fish market, more like it.

"So you bought the tie yourself." Nadine inched closer. "Who made it?"

Brock turned his tie over for Nadine to see the label.

"Ah. Versace. Good taste." On his staff salary.

Brock patted down the tie onto his pressed oxford.

"I like it. May I get a photo of it? Just the tie," Nadine said, fishing for her iPhone.

"You mean my face is not handsome enough for your camera?"

"Well, I guess I can take a picture of your chin as well."

He laughed. And posed.

Nadine took several shots. She showed him what she had taken. "You're seriously photogenic."

"I've been told that, yes," Brock concurred.

Nadine stepped back. "What time is it? Aren't we supposed to get back to the meeting?"

Brock shrugged. "We'll be fine. More water?"

"One more bottle. Thanks."

As Brock went to the refrigerator, Nadine quickly emailed the photos to Ming with a little note attached about the watch, the tie, and the possible connection to a certain Hot Dupree ex-employee.

~

"*T*he meeting resumed fifteen minutes ago," Dante Dupree snapped. He was in a dark mood as he watched Nadine slip onto her chair some three feet away.

Why wouldn't he be grumpy? Couldn't she tell?

He had seen Nadine walk out of the conference room with Brock Tennyson during a supposedly brief break. They had been gone awhile. And they had returned together.

Together!

"We were"—Brock cleared his throat—"uh, busy."

Busy? Busy doing what?

Dante wanted to slam the table with his fist, but he knew that would hurt his bones more than the table.

He eyed Nadine. She sat there looking prim and proper, sipping water as if nothing had happened.

Maybe nothing had happened.

But that's Brock Tennyson we're talking about.

Chelsea had told him about Brock's bad-boy reputation. It would be in Nadine's best interest to stay away from such a person, especially since he had a slew of classic Kawasakis and Harleys in his collection.

The last thing Dante wanted to see was Nadine on the backseat of any of Brock's bikes.

No way.

He fumed as a message came through his iPhone.

Are you mad at me?

It was from Nadine.

He refused to respond. He read on though.

Expect a text from Ming.

Dante wondered what that was about.

Ming? Ming Wei, the investigator? What for?

Dante still refused to reply to Nadine's message. He flipped his iPhone upside down so the screen rested on the table.

There, Nadine. That's my protest!

For the rest of the hour, Dante's mind was distracted to the point of a headache. Thank God Dad was around to pick up his slack.

If he were to be the future Hot Dupree CEO, he'd better be able to compartmentalize his emotions.

But Nadine...

What's happening to me?

Dante was unable to focus. All he could think about was seeing Brock and Nadine together.

Brock and Nadine walking out of the conference room.

Together.

Brock and Nadine returning to the conference room.

Together.

And it made a difference because...

Dante had no idea.

He had a feeling he should see if Ming had sent him a note, now that his curiosity had been aroused, but he wasn't about to give in and turn over his iPhone.

A gentle tap on his shoulder made him go rigid. It was Nadine's fingers.

He could feel her breath on his ear as she whispered, "Please adjourn the meeting."

Dante's eyes were on hers.

"Now?" he mouthed.

Nadine nodded.

Somehow he trusted her.

CHAPTER TWENTY

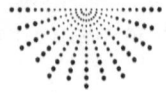

*W*hen Nadine arrived at the Dupree-Cargill beach house on Tybee Island to scoop Bradley's cat litter early Friday morning, both Dante and Abilene were waiting for her.

Dante was sitting in a recliner with his legs propped up. His sister was coming out of the kitchen with a cup of something.

They looked pleased to see her. It was comforting to Nadine because she had been missing her parents and could use friendly company.

Dad was still in Cancun, trying to score a meeting with Mom.

"You just saved Hot Dupree almost three billion dollars," Dante declared.

"Seriously?" Nadine's jaw dropped.

"Turned out that Brock Tennyson talked too much."

"Yeah, he did, but Versace and Patek Philippe also spoke," Abilene added.

"Something about money, isn't it? Root of all evil."

Is Dante trying to quote the Bible?

Nadine cleared her throat and wondered how to put it. She knew I Timothy 6:10 by heart and had applied it to her company.

For the love of money is a root of all kinds of evil, for which some have strayed from the faith in their greediness, and pierced themselves through with many sorrows.

"Am I right?" Dante asked her.

"Well, it's actually the love of money that's the root of all evil. Money is amoral, a thing, a tool. Just like a brick or stone. Lifeless. But in the hands of people, money reveals the intentions of the human heart."

Dante didn't say anything.

"I'm sorry."

"About what, Nadine?"

"For correcting you."

Dante smiled. "You can correct me all you want. As long as you only speak the truth to me."

"I will always speak the truth to you, Dante."

"Sounds like a vow." Dante chuckled.

Nadine looked horrified.

Abilene laughed as she approached the two of them. She placed the hot cup in Dante's hand. To Nadine, she said, "Want something? Coffee? Tea?"

"Nothing. Thank you." Nadine found Bradley walking about and scooped him up.

"You must have put Brock quite at ease for him to say all that to you about Chelsea," Dante said.

"He didn't specifically mention her name, you know." Nadine hugged Bradley.

"I know. But it was a brilliant move to contact Ming. There were too many electronic transfers between Chelsea and Brock. It was unmistakable what they had been doing behind my back."

"But you'll need more evidence, Dante."

"It's a start. Ming is on it. Sadly, Coastal Condiments was only a conduit for a third party to invade Hot Dupree."

"I won't ask you what company that is, but Brock said something about bigger things."

Dante nodded. "It's amazing how you recalled that entire conversation."

"I wish I had recorded it on my iPhone instead of having to write it out," Nadine said. She had done so as soon as she reached home the night before. She had sent off her statement to Ming, with a copy to Dante.

"We have enough to go on." Dante's voice sounded kind.

"Good." Nadine sat down with Bradley. The cat purred in her arms.

Abilene eased onto the seat next to Nadine in the living room. "Something we can do for you in return?"

"No need. You've done enough. If Dad and Mom get back together again, I'll have Dante to thank."

"Don't thank me. Thank God," Dante added. "Only He can fix a marriage."

It was unmistakable, this change. Nadine wondered what went on in his head.

And heart.

One moment, he had skipped church, and another, he had remembered God. At least he was maturing spiritually, and that ought to be applauded, right?

"Nadine, we want to do something for you." Abilene stroked her round belly.

"Not necessary, friend."

Bradley broke free from Nadine's arms, apparently done with all that cuddling. He lumbered off to find a streak of morning sun on a rug by the door to the terrace, and promptly went to sleep.

"How about dinner with me?" Dante asked.

Abilene laughed. "That's so inadequate, big Brother. I was thinking more along the lines of paying off Nadine's mortgage."

"Oh, I already paid it off," Nadine said.

"That's cool. What about car payments?"

"All gone." Nadine was all smiles. "No student loans either. You remember I worked throughout my years at SCAD."

"Yeah. Took you an extra two years, but you made it out. If not for that, we wouldn't have met."

"Those were the carefree days, Abilene." Nadine leaned over to hug her friend. She felt something kick her elbow. "Whoa."

"Want to feel my baby?" Abilene asked.

Nadine nodded. She glanced over at Dante, who seemed to be amused at the exchange between the two women.

Slowly, Nadine placed her hand on Abilene's tummy. She could feel a little kick against her palm. "Oooh. Feisty."

"That's at four months in my womb," Abilene said. "Imagine what she's going to do when she turns four years old and runs around. She'll be like Uncle Dante over there. Can't sit still."

Well, ironically, Dante didn't move in his recliner.

He was staring at Nadine.

"Uncle Dante." Nadine repeated what Abilene had called him. "It does have a nice ring to it."

Dante didn't say a word.

"Seriously, Nadine," Abilene continued. "What can we do for you?"

"Maybe you can pray for my parents. They need a lot of prayer."

"Yes, I promise to do that," Abilene said. "But non-prayer things to compensate for your help. Hot Dupree is forever in your debt, Nadine."

"God is good."

"Yes, He is. And for such a time as this, here you are." Abilene leaned back. "Do you want to expand your VA company?"

"That." Nadine groaned. "My clients want too much from me."

"I know," Abilene said.

"Your brother has given me some ideas."

"Like what?"

"Increase my rates. Filter prospective clients. Hire minions."

"Those are good ideas." To Dante, Abilene gave two thumbs up.

Dante nodded slightly. He sipped his coffee.

Nadine was aware that he was still watching her. The awareness was affecting how she thought and responded to the conversation.

The sooner she got out of here, the better.

"Speaking of work, I have to get going." Nadine eased off the sofa. "Time to scoop the litter."

Abilene tried to get up with great difficulty.

Nadine gave her a hand.

They laughed.

"It'll be your turn someday." Abilene wagged a finger at Nadine.

"I would love to have kids one day, but it may never happen." Oops. Nadine couldn't retract it now. "Too busy, you know."

"Too busy for love and marriage?" Abilene asked.

Before Nadine could answer her, she felt too aware of Dante's presence in the room even though he hadn't spoken a word since Nadine and his sister had discussed babies.

Nadine took a deep breath. *Need some damage control.* "Too busy to chat when I need to scoop litter and scoot out of here."

"Ah, avoiding the topic," Dante said.

"I'm not." Nadine walked closer to Dante. "And I'm not afraid of you."

"I don't want you to be afraid of me. I want you to—umm... Say, why don't I buy you dinner to thank you for saving Hot Dupree from a merger disaster?"

"There's no need."

"Absolutely, I want to."

"You're persistent." Nadine laughed.

"Are you witnessing this, Abilene?" Dante pushed a button on his recliner to lower the footrest. "She said yes."

"I only said you're persistent," Nadine protested.

"Sounds like a *yes* to me."

"No, it's not."

"Then you would have said *no*."

"I did. I said *no need*." Nadine's shoulders slacked. *Can't win this.* "All right, if you want to do something, how about a donation to the Riverside Chapel building fund? We're still trying to buy a church building."

"Now that's a great idea." Abilene pushed Dante's wheelchair to him. She put it on park, and Dante hoisted himself onto the wheelchair. He adjusted his legs.

Nadine thought she could do that—

Do what?

Well, help Dante get in and out of his wheelchair, of course.

But why? What for?

He's going home this weekend, and I won't see him again.

"And go to dinner with me." Dante's waiting eyes were on Nadine.

Nadine was trying to find another way to say *no*,

but she couldn't think of anything to say when her heart said *maybe*.

He was nice to be with and had a pleasant disposition and yet...

Abilene turned to Nadine. "Would you humor my silly old brother, go out with him, and put him out of his misery? Just one time?"

CHAPTER TWENTY-ONE

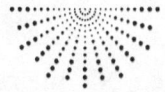

"What did she say?" Nadine adjusted the microphone on her headset. She closed the blinds facing her backyard, blocking out the afternoon sun.

This would be a good day for swimming.

Yeah, for anyone else.

As for her, she had to work to pay the bills and to accumulate retirement income. Sure, she wasn't quite thirty years old yet, but one could never be too prepared.

"Dad, I can barely hear you." Nadine waited as Dad said he was walking around wherever he was to get better reception on his cell phone.

Dad regaled her with the story of how he had tracked down Mom—with the help of Ming's contacts in Cancun—and somehow managed to invite her out to dinner on the beach.

"I can't wait to get extra cheese on mine," Dad said.

"Extra what?"

"Cheese. You know I like lots of cheese on my pizza."

"Stop right there." Nadine rubbed her forehead. "Did you say pizza?"

"Your mom likes pizza!" Dad's voice boomed into Nadine's earpiece.

"Let me get this straight. You're both in Cancun. Kind of a romantic setting there. And you invited her to dinner under the moonlight, perhaps."

"Right."

"But."

"But?"

"You're ordering pizza!" Nadine sighed. "Even I could tell you that's a bad idea. I, who don't date much!"

"Except for that idiot you brought to the house last year. He was lying through his teeth about being an artist."

"He's history."

"Yeah. Art history. Get it?" Dad laughed.

"Dad, be serious. That was in the past. We have a present problem. If you invited Mom to dinner on the beach, then take my advice. Do. Not. Order. Pizza."

"Why not? Pizza's easy. Besides, I like pepperoni."

"You know that Mom doesn't like pepperoni. She likes Hawaiian."

"She'll learn to like pepperoni."

Nadine breathed in slowly, composing her thoughts. "This might be part of the problem."

"Pizza is never a problem, my sweet daughter."

"If she hasn't liked pepperoni in forty years, she's probably not going to learn to like it the next forty years."

"She can order other toppings."

"Yes, but there's a time and place for every-thing." Nadine paced back and forth in her tiny living room.

"Don't tell us what to do, child."

Nadine stopped pacing. When Dad called her a child, something was up. "What's going on?"

"Your mom is driving me nuts. Can't think straight."

"Let's pray and ask God for a calm spirit and wisdom, okay?"

"Sure. You go ahead."

"All right." Nadine sat down in a rocker by the window. It had been salvaged from an estate sale. It was very old and had dovetail notches and nicks.

She often wondered how many people had sat in it, praying for others, for God's mercy and grace.

"Dear Lord Jesus, You are sovereign over Mom and Dad. You saw this coming, and You have allowed it for a reason. I pray for beautiful weather for this special dinner my parents will be having on the beach. I pray for peace and harmony between Mom and Dad. I pray that You will solve their problems. In Jesus' Name. Amen."

"And dear Lord," Dad began. "Please don't let any sand get into our pepperoni pizza tomorrow night."

CHAPTER TWENTY-TWO

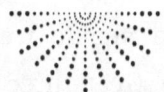

hen Nadine had insisted she didn't want to go anywhere fancy, she realized she was just like Dad. The day before, she had chided Dad for inviting Mom to dinner for two on the beaches of Cancun, and ordering pizza.

And here she was, asking Dante not to take her to any five-star James Beard restaurant in Savannah, telling him that she preferred soup, salad, and a sandwich at Piper's Place.

I am my father's daughter.

She wondered now what Dante thought of her as he sat across from her at the table. The server had removed two chairs so that Dante could roll his wheelchair all the way to the table's edge.

All around them, the tables were filled. It was a busy Saturday evening at Piper's, as usual.

Nadine found it amusing that Dante continued to peer at the five-page menu of all dishes southern and fusion. He had been quiet for a good minute.

Nadine looked outside the windows, scrubbed clean and clear. The Talmadge Memorial Bridge sparkled across the water. The sky was clear, the moon was out, and people were strolling on the riverfront across the street, three floors down.

Dante put down his menu. "Lots to choose from."

"They're open twenty-four seven, so you can choose breakfast at midnight and lunch at daybreak, if you want."

"And you've tried them all?"

"When I was in college, I practically lived here." Nadine adjusted the menu on the table. "I worked in the kitchen some."

"You cooked?"

"No. I wish I could. I did the dishes and cleaned up the place. Janitorial stuff." She waited to see if that fazed Dante.

He simply continued. "Tell me you didn't do that for four years."

"No. In my junior and senior years, I worked for a fashion magazine, proofing copies and copyediting and such. I worked on their website content."

"And thus you paid your way through college."

"But you already knew that." Nadine sipped

mineral water. No caffeinated drinks for her this evening. Saturday night was her night to go to bed early. She didn't want to miss Sunday School in the morning.

After church, she had planned on going through her yard to see what Dad had scattered. At the back of her mind, she could just imagine those iron and steel and metal pieces cutting up her lawnmower. She wished Dad had rented a storage unit. He had thrown his junk into her yard without even asking her.

But Dad was going through a trial.

Nadine knew she had to give him mercy as God had given her mercy over the years.

Who knows? Maybe Dad will get saved this year.

"Hello?" Dante asked.

"Huh?" Nadine snapped to attention.

"Lost you for a moment."

"Sorry."

"I'm poor company."

"You're not, Dante. I just have a lot on my mind."

The server came and went.

"You only ordered a single sandwich," Dante complained. "I can afford soup and salad too, you know."

"Well, I thought I wanted salad and a sandwich, but I ate a late lunch, and... So sorry I ruined our dinner. I shouldn't have insisted on coming here."

"I like it here. I like the atmosphere." Dante waved his fingers. "For a place this busy, this table is pretty private. And the view is gorgeous."

"You're kind."

"Am I?" Dante splayed his hands on the table. "You're the one who's kind, Nadine. You didn't even want to go out with me. This dinner is nothing compared to what you've done for me, saving Hot Dupree from the fire."

"God did it."

"Yeah, but He chose to work through you."

"Will you go to church with me Sunday?" Nadine blurted. Horrified at what came out of her mouth, she retracted it. "Don't come to church with me. I mean, go to church if you want, but not because of me. Do it because of God."

"Why is church that important to you?" Dante pushed aside his sweet tea as the server brought his salad. "If we have God, isn't that enough?"

"Yes, God is all we need. And yet the Bible says not to forsake coming together for congregational worship." Nadine searched her Bible app on her iPad, which automatically connected to the restaurant's Wi-Fi.

"Let me read what Hebrews 10:25 says."

...not forsaking the assembling of ourselves together, as is the manner of some, but exhorting one another, and so much the more as you see the Day approaching.

Dante didn't seem convinced. "Churches these days are full of politics and bickering."

"Not all churches. Riverside Chapel is not like that. Pastor Flores is a good shepherd."

"I've been there once."

"I'm not saying it's perfect, but I'm saying that our church tries to obey God."

"Good for you all."

"You're a Christian. Which church do you attend?"

"My parents' church whenever I'm home. I'm not home most of the time."

"It's hard to travel and attend church. What about watching your pastor online? Pastor Flores, for example, does live broadcasts of all his sermons."

Dante nodded. "I have to tell you the truth. I used to go to church more. After what happened to me, I'm not sure if I like the way God has arranged my life. I'll never walk again, and this is my new normal."

"God has allowed the accident. I don't believe He caused it." Nadine waited for the server to come and go. "Would you like to say grace?"

"Sure." Dante prayed a very short prayer.

It's okay. At least he thanked God for the food.

"You said God allowed my paralysis." Dante reached for the salt and pepper.

Nadine nodded. "We don't know why God allowed it. Every sowing has a reaping, and the repercussions can affect innocent people."

"If I hadn't run for a touchdown, I wouldn't be a paraplegic today."

"You are your legs, and your legs are you." Nadine raised her eyebrows. "Is that correct?"

"Of course not! I'm not even a leg model." Dante laughed. "What are you talking about?"

"But you talked like your entire life is below the waist." Nadine placed the cloth napkin on her lap. She lifted up the sourdough bread to look underneath. She pulled out the pieces of raw onions they'd stuck in her sandwich. She had forgotten to tell them to hold the onions.

"You don't like onions," Dante said.

"Not if they're raw. I like my onions cooked. But what I like to eat doesn't define me." Nadine smiled. "How you move from place to place doesn't define you."

"That's a stretch. How did you get from food to walking?"

"Mouth, feet, body parts. Get it? If I were

missing an arm, would I still be me? If you can't walk, are you still you?"

"If you put it that way, I guess I was wrong." Dante dug into his hamburger.

"I'm trying to make a point that parts of us do not make the whole," Nadine said. "What about the rest of you? What's in your heart, your mind, your soul?"

"There's a verse I used to memorize back in high school and college." Dante paused. "Before this."

"What verse is it?"

"Galatians 2:20."

"One of my favorites." Nadine waited. She hoped that Dante could remember it. If not, she wasn't sure it was her place to help him remember.

"You're waiting for me to tell you what it says." Dante put down his hamburger.

"You can eat first."

"No. You want to know what's going on with me."

"Well..."

Dante wiped his fingers on a napkin. He logged into his iPhone. "Ready?"

Nadine nodded.

"Galatians 2:20 says, 'I have been crucified with Christ; it is no longer I who live, but Christ lives in me; and the life which I now live in the flesh I live by faith in the Son of God, who loved me and gave

Himself for me.' I used to be able to recite this verse."

"But what does it mean to you?"

"In Christ. My life is in Christ." Dante said the words so quietly that Nadine almost didn't hear him. "My life is not in my paralysis."

CHAPTER TWENTY-THREE

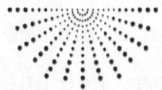

"*W*here are you in all this?" Nadine asked as they strolled along the waterfront.

The Savannah River glimmered in the moon-light. Across the river, Hutchinson Island was dark except for the hotel lights. The bridge was behind them, and two riverboats were in front of them.

One of the riverboats housed Riverside Chapel. A lot had happened the previous couple of years at Riverside Chapel. Even their own pastor had found his true love. Pastor Flores and Heidi had been married on the riverboat, as had Abilene and Lars in their surprise wedding.

That was the first real time Nadine had paid any serious attention to Dante. He had been off limits even then.

But he wasn't dating now.

"Me?" Dante wheeled forward, keeping up with Nadine.

Or was it Nadine keeping up with Dante?

"Yes, you." Nadine stood in front of Dante. She had purposely worn flat shoes tonight so that she didn't tower over him. He had long legs, and Nadine guessed that if he were standing up, he'd be over six feet tall. Sitting down, he had to look up to Nadine, and she didn't like that. She preferred to be at eye level with him.

After all, she had enjoyed their talk at Piper's Place, and she wanted more conversation.

Dante looked a bit tired though. They'd have to go home soon.

She glanced around, and spotted Waylon sitting on a bench eating a cupcake. She waved to him. He simply nodded.

A chaperone.

"Where are you, Dante Dupree, in that world of yours?" Nadine asked again.

"What do you mean?"

"Under the pile of men's accolades, where is the real you?"

"I'm here."

"Not the future CEO Dante, the charming Dante, the kind and generous Dante. Those are

things you do." Nadine smiled. "Where is the man
to whom God has given life?"

Dante looked like he was about to say something
but decided against it.

"I want to see that Dante. Until then, this is stuff
and fluff."

Dante laughed heartily. "Stuff and fluff? You
call my life fluffy?"

Nadine knew what he had implied.

Well, I'm not calling his billions fluff.

Not exactly.

"Men's medals. Men's successes. Men's whatever. They are all from men," Nadine explained.
"Where is the real you?"

Dante parked his wheelchair. He stretched out
a hand to Nadine, his palm up.

Nadine wasn't sure what he was up to, but she
placed her hand in his. His hand was warm, very
warm.

Dante pulled her toward himself. He patted his
lap with his other hand. "By invitation only."

"Really?" Nadine raised an eyebrow.

"I can't feel anyone sitting on my lap, so it's off
limits, except for my little nieces and nephews,
family cats, and now you."

"What about all the wom—sorry."

"All the women I ever dated the last several

years?" Dante chuckled. "Photo ops. Nothing goes on behind closed doors. And no, they have not sat on my lap."

"Really." It wasn't a question.

"What does that mean?"

"What?"

"You said *really*. Does that mean you believe me? Or are you being sarcastic?"

Nadine smiled. "Remember the day I was looking for Bradley? We bantered over another word."

"Sure."

"I believe that was the word."

"Exactly, Nadine. And you said that 'God holds us accountable for what comes out of our mouths.'"

"You remembered."

"I remember everything about us."

Us? Nadine wondered what Dante was getting at.

Dante patted his thighs again. His eyes invited her.

Slowly, carefully so as not to hurt him, Nadine sat down on his lap. They were almost eye to eye.

They stayed there that way, the two of them, staring at each other in the warm August night.

Dante smiled. Then grinned like a little kid.

Nadine wasn't sure what was going through his mind, but he seemed to be happy.

"Here I am, Nadine. Just Dante," he said as he wrapped his arms around her.

Nadine snuggled into his chest. His chest was warm. His arms were warm.

When Nadine looked up, he seemed to be waiting for something.

"Nadine," Dante finally spoke.

"Yes?"

"I have a question for you."

"Sure."

"*Sure* as in 'ask away,' or *sure* as in 'everybody has a question'?"

"Must you parse everything I say?" Nadine curled her arms around Dante's neck and shoulders.

"Every word is important, right? You told me that." A wind came over the river and tugged at Dante's curly hair, pushing his locks about. Some of it fell over his forehead.

Nadine reached up and touched his hair ever so slightly.

He didn't move and didn't make a sound.

Nadine's lips curled into a smile as she tipped them toward his unmoving lips. Gently, lightly, Nadine savored his warm lips.

Dante responded, running warm hands up and down her back and pulling her closer to him as he finished her kiss for her.

Soon, Nadine tipped her head back. "That's the answer. Now what's your question?"

"This." And he kissed her again.

CHAPTER TWENTY-FOUR

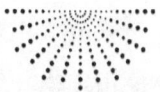

"*W*ell, what do you think?" Abilene asked Dante as they left the Sunday morning worship service at Riverside Chapel.

Lars was behind Abilene, and he carried her Bible and purse for her. Around them, people were chatting, walking, leaving.

"Of Pastor Flores?" Dante knew Abilene was up to something.

"Of what he said regarding sanctification after salvation?" Abilene stepped out of the dining room.

Dante followed her. He had been to Riverside Chapel once before, and he remembered coming up the ramp earlier this morning, but it seemed easier to just follow Abilene.

"That. Well, I agree somewhat, but it seems like a lot of work to be constantly trying to get right with God, do the right thing, and all that."

"Ah, that's why we have the Holy Spirit to teach us and help us."

Dante didn't respond to that. He knew what Abilene was talking about, what she was trying to remind him of. It was just that it had been too long since he had stopped responding to the promptings of the Holy Spirit.

Who could blame him, right? For fourteen years, he had been in this wheelchair. Where had God been all those fourteen years?

Sometimes Dante felt like God had abandoned him.

"God is always there for you, even if you forget him," Abilene said in her cheery voice.

Did I forget God? Abandon Him instead of the other way around?

"I don't want to argue with you," Dante replied. "But I hate for our Sunday conversation to be what you might brand as teachable moments."

"Every day is a day to learn, isn't it?" Abilene smiled. "Especially Sunday. That's why we have Sunday School, and that's why we call Pastor Flores a teaching pastor."

"If it makes you feel any better, I'll listen to his

sermon again." Dante wheeled down the ramp. "And that would be twice today. Afraid we can't say the same about Nadine. She wasn't even in the service."

Abilene turned toward Dante. It seemed she had to turn her entire body just to make eye contact with him. Was it just his imagination, or had Abilene's tummy grown a lot bigger in one week?

"That's because she was in the nursery," Abilene explained. "We all take turns so that moms can attend the service. So we miss one Sunday morning service every quarter. Don't worry about Nadine. She'll listen to the sermon this afternoon. She always does when she has to be in the nursery."

For some reason, Dante spun his wheelchair around so he could look back at the riverboat.

And there she was. Nadine on deck, carrying a baby.

The sight was not lost on him.

She handed the baby over to Sabine Wei, whom Dante had recognized as Ming's wife. Dante had run into him in church this morning, and they had discussed the investigations that Ming was doing for Hot Dupree. While they had been chatting, Ming's wife showed up to say hello.

Speaking of whom, Ming now appeared next to his wife, and there they were, a lovely couple, standing on the deck of Riverside Chapel, with their six-month-old baby.

Somehow it broke Dante's heart into a million shards.

CHAPTER TWENTY-FIVE

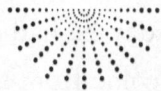

omething had changed between Dante and her this weekend. Whether it was good or bad, Nadine wasn't sure.

She had finished lunch on her back porch while listening to one of Pastor Flores's recorded sermons. She was about to go back to work when she felt an urgent need to pray.

Pastor Flores had said in his sermon this morning that God's Word sanctified Christians.

Sanctify them by Your truth. Your word is truth.

The Lord Jesus Christ's prayer in John 17:17 was for believers. That fact swirled in Nadine's head as she tossed the paper plate into the trash can.

She didn't feel like doing dishes this afternoon,

hence all these paper products. It helped that she could buy paper plates to feed a thousand at Sam's Club. They weren't going to run out of them anytime soon.

She turned off the porch fan and adjourned to her bedroom, where she and Dad had moved her office table the first day he had arrived to stay with her. The table had come from the only other room in the house, a guest bedroom that Nadine had turned into a small home office. They had cleared out that even smaller room for Dad to sleep in.

Nadine had wanted to give Dad some privacy even though he had said he wouldn't mind sleeping on the couch. The last thing Nadine wanted was to hear snoring from the living room, right outside her bedroom.

So she had given Dad her home office. A futon sufficed as his bed. At a thrift shop, Dad had found a nightstand and a table lamp to go with it. Nadine thought he had done well.

If only Mom were here to enjoy all of Dad's finds.

Those two had been married for decades. And now this.

Nadine wondered whether her own future marriage could last.

Well, in Jesus, all things were possible.

"Lord, I want You to sanctify me today and

clarify my thoughts. What happened between Dante and me on Friday night seemed so natural, and yet, I'm not sure if it will go anywhere."

A tear fell.

"Lord, forgive me. I didn't mean to be an easy catch for him. He told me to sit on his lap. I did. And I kissed him first. But I realized later that he had wanted to kiss me too."

Nadine wiped her face. She was very glad she could talk to God like this, with honesty, pouring out her heart, with no one else around her to question her emotions.

"Please clarify my thoughts, and sanctify me." Nadine repeated her prayer, more to reason with herself that, if God showed her what to do, then all would be well, and she would be on the right path.

Would the right path be alongside Dante?

He had said that no other women had sat on his lap. What did that mean?

He had said that all those women he had been seen with had been for photo ops.

Why? To appear popular?

Perhaps Dante was a lonely man, after all.

Well, I'm lonely too.

She wished she had a cat to talk to, but as long as Dad was staying with her, cats were out.

Nadine reached for a tissue paper box nearby. She blew her nose, and then closed her eyes.

"Lord Jesus, I wait for Your answer to my prayer. In Your Holy Name I pray. Amen."

Time to get some work done before the evening service.

Nadine scanned through her emails for the day. Waddell wanted this. Waddell wanted that. Waddell wanted more than this poor virtual assistant could provide.

Nadine wondered whether she should hire an assistant.

How funny! A virtual assistant with an assistant of her own.

Pretty soon, Nadine was so engrossed in preparing the itinerary for Waddell's tour in Eastern Europe—he had added to his plans at the last minute—that she didn't hear Dad come into her room until he was standing right beside her.

She screamed, palms to her chest. "Dad! You scared me. I didn't hear you."

"I had the cab drop me off at the front of the subdivision."

Uh-oh. The walk.

It meant Dad had a heavy heart and needed to walk it off.

Nadine could have picked him up at the Savannah/Hilton Head International Airport, where Dad had flown in on a one-way commercial airline ticket.

But when Dad had insisted on taking the cab,

who was she to tell him what to do when his life—primarily, his marriage—had spiraled out of control? Far be it for Nadine to take away more decision-making from Dad only to save on cab fare.

Dad's worn duffel bag slid to the old carpet floor. He plopped down at the edge of Nadine's twin bed. He looked like he had been crying.

Nadine tried not to glance at her computer screen, but she had left at least seven or eight windows opened at various travel agencies and hotel sites. They would all have to wait.

Dad needed her.

And that was the way it went. Nadine would drop anything and everything for her family.

"It didn't work out." Dad shook his head. "It was a wasted trip."

"Nothing is ever wasted if God is working it out."

"God again. You always talk about God, as if He can solve all my problems."

"He sure can," Nadine said.

"What? All I have to do is believe?"

"Well, believe in Jesus Christ, all of Him, what He represents. I'm not talking about shallow, facetious belief, as if you can just ask God for whatever you want and you're going to get it. Like they say, God is not a genie in a bottle or a button on a vending machine."

Dad moaned. "I could use a miracle right now. I've lost Soledad."

"Fortunately for you, God works miracles, and nothing is impossible for God."

"That so?"

"Yep."

"Then you'd better pray to your God about your mom, because I counted at least four or five pairs of ogling eyes on her when I was in Cancun." Dad shook his head. "It must be that bright, hot lime-green swimsuit she was wearing. Or her smile. Soledad always has a nice smile. You have her smile, you know."

Nadine tried to keep her emotions together. *Think of God.* "We'll pray that God will restore your marriage, and bring her back to us."

"You'd better pray fast, Nadine. This is 911." Dad started to sob. "And you were right. She still hates pepperoni. She wanted me to cook her a hamburger. How was I going to do that in Cancun without my grill?"

CHAPTER TWENTY-SIX

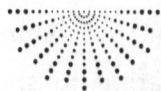

*N*adine made it to the Sunday evening service at Riverside Chapel, then rushed home to take care of her clients' needs. She had to stop taking clients in different time zones if she were to get any sleep at all. It had begun as a way to make income. Speakers in demand often paid her more than other clients.

Yet, it didn't make sense anymore. Take Waddell, for example. He was the ultimate historian, lecturing on-site, writing books, and promoting them everywhere. Nadine had her friend, Heidi, to thank for this client who had taught European history at the University of Georgia, where Heidi had attended in her undergraduate years. That was, until he had been bitten by the travel bug.

Yep. The man wasn't coming home to the United States any time soon.

Nadine had worked all night, doing anything Waddell needed. She was paid by the hour, but it was six o'clock in the morning, and she hadn't slept. She had prepared Waddell's lecture slides for him, and at this moment, five hours away in Warsaw, Waddell was preparing to speak at a university there.

Behind the scene, she had helped make it happen. Waddell had paid her a bonus for that. The money had just arrived. That meant she could afford to have Dad stay with her.

Life is good. All good.

Thank You, Lord.

She collapsed on top of the comforter on her bed. She couldn't go to sleep. Her adrenaline was way up there. Also, there were two more clients to take care of before noon.

One was Twitter phobic and the other was Facebook challenged. It was Nadine's job to take care of their social media for them. For those two, she also updated their websites and proofread any content they wanted her to post.

Nadine didn't mind doing those things as long as she was paid.

And pay her they did.

She wondered sometimes if she was overpaid.

Banish the thought!

She had done exactly what they had hired her to do: be their online assistant for whatever they needed. Most of the time it was scheduling, keeping them organized. She had been surprised at how disorganized some of her clients could be.

That's why they hired me.

Her job was to assist them, get them going, keep them afloat, save them some trouble.

Yeah, like the way she had assisted Dante and rescued him from a bad merger deal.

She still couldn't believe that all it had taken was to listen to a gabber from Coastal Condiments shoot his mouth off about stealing employees from Hot Dupree.

For some reason, thinking about Dante and Hot Dupree plastered a smile on Nadine's face.

"A penny for your smile?"

Nadine nearly jumped up. She rolled over on the bed. Dad was standing at the door.

"The door is open," Dad defended himself. "Is he cute?"

"What?"

"Not what, Nadine. Who?"

Dad leaned against the doorframe. "Does he treat you with respect?"

Nadine nodded.

"Speaks the truth?"

"I think so."

"Better be sure."

"He's a Christian too."

"Even Christians lie."

Nadine nodded. Yes, Dad was right. Even Christians lied.

"So bring him here."

Nadine sighed. "He lives in New Orleans."

"But he was here in Savannah recently."

"He went home last night." At evening church the night before, Abilene had told Nadine that Dante was on a flight home to Louisiana.

Nadine had received a text message from him later saying he had arrived safely. He was going to be busy for a few weeks, but he would keep in touch.

"Next time he comes to town, bring him here," Dad said.

"Oh no, Dad. No interrogations."

"Interview."

"I'm not in high school anymore."

"You're my only daughter." Dad sat down on Nadine's swivel chair. "You'll always be my baby. You know that. What's his name?"

"Dante. Abilene Dupree's brother." Nadine sat up on her bed and crossed her legs. "Do you remember Abilene?"

"Yeah, the artist. Your classmate at SCAD." Dad's eyes were on Nadine.

Uh-oh. "What?"

"When do I meet this Dante fellow?"

"Soon."

"Don't do anything I wouldn't do."

"Dad! You know me better than that."

Dad paused. He looked like he was deep in thought. "You know, maybe your God does protect you after all."

"That's my God. Always my protector. You don't have to worry. God has my back."

Dad nodded. "Want some breakfast?"

"What are we having?"

"Eggs."

"Eggs? We're out of eggs." Nadine didn't remember buying eggs and milk this week. They had to have been out of those for a couple of days. She felt bad she had been working all weekend.

"I bought eggs," Dad declared.

"When?"

"Last night when you were at church. They were on sale."

"How many dozens?"

"In a carton."

"Carton? Those aren't real eggs, Dad."

"It says egg substitute."

"I want real eggs for breakfast. Let's go to Waffle

House. Then we can stop at Publix on the way home. How does that sound?"

Dad stood up. "Sounds like I'd better drive. From the looks of it, you didn't sleep all night. Am I right?"

"My clients..."

"You'd better find new clients before they run you to the ground. If you don't get enough sleep, you'll get old quick."

Nadine didn't answer. "Give me fifteen minutes. I'm going to brush my teeth and take a quick shower."

"Okay. I'll go make a grocery list. I saw the Sunday papers. Nuggets are on sale."

"What kind of nuggets?"

"The frozen ones. What other nuggets are there? They're on sale for seventy percent off if we get them today."

"There's a reason they're on sale." Nadine stretched. "Put on the list whatever else we need to get, okay? Cereal, soda, toilet paper, whatever household items you think we need."

"Wish your mom were here. She makes that sort of list."

"When she comes back, she can stay here too." Nadine sucked in her tears.

Lord, You have to bring Mom back. Dad is dying here.

Dad was leaving the room, when he stopped abruptly. "I don't want to put you out."

"No. I just got paid."

"And just so you know, I am abiding by your house rules."

"Thank you." Nadine had seen him sneak out to his Volkswagen van every now and then to raid his small refrigerator.

That was the way it went if Dad wanted to continue living in her house. No alcohol allowed. If he wanted his booze, he had to go out to his van and sit there until he was finished.

Still, in the last several days, Nadine had noticed that Dad hadn't been drinking as much as he used to. He had spent more time working on his junk—er, works of art—in the front yard.

Nadine felt it was good for Dad to keep busy.

Getting Mom back was one thing.

But most of all, Nadine wanted Dad to meet Jesus. Dad's whole life and future path would completely change if he met Jesus. She knew so because hers had.

She was very glad that Dante had made it to church on Sunday morning. It seemed to her that he was making an effort to get right with God and to restore the broken fellowship he had with Him.

According to Abilene, Dante was a Christian. However, many years of being unable to walk had made him bitter and caustic toward God, as if God were to blame.

Dante hadn't said that much to her, but Abilene had told her all these things long before Dante had come to town and captured her heart.

Nadine decided to put Dante on her prayer list.

Right after her parents' names.

CHAPTER TWENTY-SEVEN

"*Y*ou live in the middle of nowhere," Dante said as he closed his car door. He had reassembled his wheelchair and hoisted himself into it before Nadine came running out of her front door. "Took me an hour to get here from Tybee."

"Was traffic bad?" Nadine asked.

"Always bad on Fridays. You look nice." He stared at her, his mind figuring out how to tell her she was half-dressed.

Well, not half-dressed as in partially clad, but she still had on an old pair of capris. The blouse looked like dinner material, but the capri pants had to go. The five-star restaurant he was going to take her tonight insisted on formal attire.

"I'm sorry I'm not ready. One of my clients

called and said she can't access her website. She went all frantic."

"So you're tech support now?" Dante asked.

"Some of my clients think I do everything." Nadine laughed. "Come inside? Dad put a ramp up at the front door for you."

"That's very kind of him, but I can wait out here." Dante glanced beyond Nadine and was glad he had decided to stay outdoors.

That plywood ramp to the front door might not hold the weight of him, though his wheelchair was light. In any case, he didn't want to risk finding out a week before the procedure.

Yes, that procedure he wouldn't tell Nadine about unless it succeeded. It was going to cost a fortune, but the surgeons in Tokyo said that there was a remote possibility it could work.

Out of the corner of his eye he spotted a sixty-something-year-old man amble out of the front door. He was a big man coming out of the tiny house half the size of Dante's garage back home.

The man walked past a ghastly looking lawn that was covered with weeds and tall grass and strewn with all sorts of rusty things.

Dante pointed out to Nadine, still standing near him. "I'll need an all-terrain wheelchair to cross that lawn."

"Tell me about it." Nadine kept her voice low. "I have my tetanus shots. Do you?"

That drew a chuckle out of Dante. He reached for her hand, but before he could get to her, Nadine's dad was staring him down.

"I'm Lloyd Saylor. You must be Dante Dupree." Big handshake.

Dante liked that. "Yes, sir. I am. Good to meet you."

"I must thank you for the flight to Cancun to find my wife."

"No problem." *I did it for Nadine.*

"I would have written you a thank-you note except my eyesight ain't so good these days, and my handwriting is even worse than my eyesight."

"Don't mention it." *Yes, I really did it for Nadine.*

Lloyd told his daughter to go inside. To get ready. "I'm going to sit here with Dante. Talk a bit."

"Dad!" Nadine looked horrified. "I'm twenty-eight years old."

"You will always be my little girl. We've established that." Lloyd made some sort of squinty eye signal to his daughter.

"Dad," Nadine protested.

Dante put warm fingers on her arm. "Go."

He watched Nadine drag herself into the house.

Amused, he turned to Lloyd. "So what do you want to talk about, sir?"

"This way, young man."

Step into my office?

Dante followed him on the cracked concrete driveway to a swing at the edge of the driveway on the other side of the garage. Lloyd sat down on the swing, facing Dante.

"I prefer Too Much Spice over Hot Dupree," Lloyd declared.

"Good to have choices, sir." Dante wondered how to sell his Hot Dupree killer hot sauce to Lloyd. "Have you considered mixing the two? You get a vinegar flavor in one, and you get the killer in the other."

"I haven't considered that."

"Try it sometime, and let me know."

"I will." Lloyd folded his arms across his big chest. "Nadine doesn't like anything too spicy or hot. She likes her food bland and tasteless."

Dante tried to keep a straight face. "She can choose bland from the menu."

"She got that from her mom." Lloyd choked up. "Me, I like spicy."

"With lots of Too Much Spice," Dante added.

"You got it."

Dante waved his arms, pointed to the yard. "You like to build things? Restore things?"

"Yep. Upcycle."

"And you sell what you make?"

"Some. Mostly I keep what I make. I make things for my wife." Lloyd cleared his throat. "Besides, I don't have to sell them. I have Social I can live on. I don't need much. A roof over my head, a place to rest, food to eat, and I'm content."

"Wish I could be content," Dante said.

"You look content."

"Most of the time, I am. But sometimes..." Dante wondered how much to say. "Sometimes, I wish I could just get up and walk."

Lloyd shrugged. "Walking is overrated."

"Yeah?"

"When you have two bad knees, you'll agree."

"I can't feel my knees or anything from the waist down."

"That's tough."

"Tell me about it."

They said nothing for a while.

"What's taking her so long?" Lloyd looked antsy.

"Maybe she's taking another call from her clients."

"Yeah, that. You know, Sunday night she worked through the night. Her client is out there in Europe wandering about, and he needs a lot of help to keep things straight."

"Nadine works hard."

"She works very hard. I don't know anyone who works harder than she does."

They seemed to have run out of things to say.

"Mr. Saylor," Dante said.

"Lloyd."

"Lloyd. I want you to know that I'm interested in your daughter, and I think there's something long-term here." Dante quickly formed his words. "But I can't give you grandkids."

"Hold on!" Lloyd almost rose from his swing. "Let's not get ahead of ourselves. I thought you two are only dating."

"Yes, sir."

Lloyd leaned back into his swing. "Don't scare me with all that grandkids talk."

"I'm going to pop the question soon." When Lloyd looked alarmed, Dante continued, "But not until after I talk with you."

"Now is as good a time as any, young man."

~

"I can give your daughter everything she wants—cash flow, a house on the beach, an island in the Caribbean, whatever." Dante breathed in deeply. The late afternoon August sun was burning hot. He was getting sweaty in his silk Marni button-down shirt.

Lloyd Saylor's eyebrows knotted together.

Dante wondered what he was thinking. "But I want you to know up front, I can't dance with Nadine, can't take a walk on the beach with her, can't pick her up if she trips at the curb..."

"I'm not worried about things like that."

"I can't carry her over the threshold, can't haul the groceries, can't reach the top shelf of the kitchen cabinets for her."

Lloyd laughed so hard that the entire swing jiggled and rattled.

"What's so funny, sir?" Dante asked.

"Ironies. Nadine is my daughter. I love her and would do anything for her."

"Sure."

"Let me tell you something, son."

Son?

"Soledad and I were well into our thirties when we realized that we had been trying for eighteen years to have a child. Meanwhile, there were many abandoned babies..." Lloyd teared up. "My wife and I said, give us one of those precious little ones. Just one. All we're asking for is one child. We'll love her and care for her the rest of our lives."

"And God answered your prayer."

Lloyd raised his eyebrows. "I guess you could

say that. Now Nadine and my wife believe in God, but until I see Him, that's a tough call for me."

"We walk by faith, not by sight."

"Sounds like something Nadine would say."

"It's in the Bible, sir."

"So that's where she got all those quotes from." Lloyd laughed.

Dante realized then that Lloyd might not be a believer. Was that another prayer burden for Nadine?

Speaking of whom, here she comes.

She had changed into a nice flowing dress, modestly long enough to cover her knees. The jewel-tone hues looked pretty on her. They brought out the color of her eyes.

Wow.

Dante's admiration was broken by Lloyd's panicky face.

Calmly, Dante said, "We'll talk again soon, sir."

"Bring her home before midnight."

"Yes, sir." Dante knew it meant they had to leave the restaurant before eleven o'clock to get Nadine back here before the stroke of midnight. But he could do it. If they had valet parking, he could time it right.

And impress Nadine's dad.

Nadine hugged her dad. "Don't wait up for me."

"Then how on earth am I going to know if you make it home by midnight?" Lloyd asked.

"Say, Lloyd?" Dante said. "I fly home tomorrow, but would you like to have lunch with me the next time I'm in town? We can continue our conversation."

"You mean you came all the way from Louisiana just to take my daughter out to dinner?"

"Yes, sir."

Lloyd fished for his wallet. He produced a folded business card. "Saylor Salvage is my business. My number's on there. Call me, and we'll figure out when we can do lunch."

"Sounds good." Dante took the oil-stained business card and inserted it carefully into his shirt pocket as though it were a badge of approval or an important backstage pass.

CHAPTER TWENTY-EIGHT

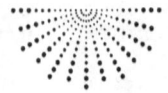

*I*t had been five weeks since Dante had attended Riverside Chapel and three weeks since they had gone out on a date. Nadine recollected how they had both talked more than they had eaten at dinner that night. They had seemed happy then.

It seemed such a quick goodbye.

Nadine was afraid it would happen. Three weeks without a single text from Dante.

Not a word.

Not a peep.

Abilene had hinted that he was out of the country. But didn't they use emails overseas? Surely.

If Dante had wanted to keep in touch, he would have.

"No news is good news?" Nadine asked aloud. "Nonsense."

It seemed like Dante had moved on.

Nadine tried not to be affected by the memories of their kisses and dinners and their brief happy times together. She tried not to think about being his flavor of the month.

While it was true that some men were like that, she had been praying and hoping that it was different for Dante and her, especially since he had said that those women photographed with him had been merely for publicity.

Especially that.

She had not shown up in any photographs with him.

Their relationship—if any—had been private.

Yeah. So private it's invisible now.

Thus, on the drive home after church this mid-September Sunday, when Nadine's iPhone buzzed with a ringtone she had designated for Dante, she nearly ran off the road and into a bridge column.

She hadn't expected him to call, and she hadn't called him, in case he needed space.

Now this.

Three words.

All he said were three words. "Leave me, Nadine."

No.

She could barely hold on to the steering wheel of her old car. She changed to the right lane and slowed down. She had forty minutes to go before she reached home—to get a few loose ends tied up before she sent her clients on their merry way—and she couldn't stop anywhere to take Dante's call.

She prayed for calm and a quiet spirit.

"Pardon me?" She asked as sweetly as possible.

"Leave me, Nadine," Dante repeated.

"No."

"I will never be able to walk you—"

"That doesn't bother me, Dante. And it hasn't affected our relationship." If they had any relationship to speak of. "You think too far ahead."

"Nadine, I care for you. I cannot *not* think about what our future could be."

Nadine grimaced. "So you cut off our present because you can't see past your humanity?"

Silence on the other end of the phone told Nadine she had struck a chord.

"It will be very hard in my condition to have a normal life."

"So you think my life is normal? I work like a dog to make ends meet. I don't think that's normal. Being with you—well, it's sort of like stress relief."

"What? I'm therapy?" Dante groaned.

"You're therapeutic."

"Good to know. I feel the same way about you. I love being with you."

"Okay, so what's the problem?" Nadine asked, stopping at a red light.

"I had a procedure done."

"Procedure? Like what procedure, exactly?" Nadine tried not to be alarmed.

She prayed again for understanding. Or maybe for God to hold her tongue so she didn't lose her cool and show her ugly side when someone said something illogical to her.

"Medical. It failed, Nadine." His voice was low, broken, dejected. "I am as you see me the rest of my life."

"I like what I see. What's the problem?"

"My spinal cord injury is permanent."

"Truth be told, I didn't think it wasn't." *There, she said it.*

"You mean you love me as I am?"

Nadine laughed. "We don't all stay as we are. We grow spiritually. If we're not growing spiritually, then we're shrinking back."

"I'm talking about my physical issues. For instance, I will probably not be able to—uh..."

"Let me stop you there, Dante."

"Yes, ma'am?"

"We're still at the dating stage. Let's not get too far ahead of ourselves."

"Right."

"What time zone are you in?" she asked.

"I'm home."

That was good enough for Nadine. She did not want to ask him what had happened, why his medical procedure didn't work, and why he was feeling downcast.

Nadine knew that Jesus was Dante's only remedy. To be in Christ was to have a full life.

That's what I wish for him, Lord.

"I'm serious, Nadine. I'm no good for you. I'm stuck."

"We're all stuck sometimes."

"I'm more stuck than others," Dante explained. "I can't go anywhere or do anything without help. I'll be dependent on you the rest of my life."

"And you find that beneath you, Sir High and Mighty?"

Silence on the phone.

"We are all needy," Nadine continued. "If we're never needy, why did Christ die for us?"

Silence.

"Regardless of whether you need me or I need you, we both need Jesus. Until our relationship with Him is in the right place, you and I will not work out."

And more silence.

At least he hasn't hung up.

Nadine knew she had to say a difficult thing next. "Don't need me, Dante. Need Jesus."

~

*A*nd that was that.

It was over.

After the phone call, Dante Dupree disappeared from Nadine's life. Her life was so busy that she had no time to figure out what had happened. All she knew was that he had stopped calling her, stopped communicating with her, and stopped further interactions with her.

Leave me, Nadine.

Nadine continued to take care of Bradley at Abilene's house, but they didn't speak of Dante until a few weeks later when Nadine brought a new bag of cat litter to the beach house. It was right after lunch, and Abilene had said she would be home all afternoon.

Abilene let her in, and after Nadine had taken care of Bradley, they went out to the terrace to get some October sun. It was still warm, but not burning hot like summer usually was in the South.

"I'm very sorry." Abilene could barely cross her legs as she sat on a cushy chair.

Abilene was six months pregnant.

"You're looking good, Abilene," Nadine said.

"Don't change the subject."

"What?"

"Dear friend, my coldhearted brother dumped you and disappeared without a trace. No contact, no closure, no care. You're telling me you don't feel it?"

"I'm numb, so numb I really don't want to care." Nadine slipped on a pair of sunglasses.

The oblique sun shone down on the sea oats to the left of her view of the ocean and sky. To the right was a patch of sand, flat as could be, where the original house had stood when Abilene and Lars first bought it. They had razed that condemned house and rebuilt a new one farther away from the ocean.

Between the dunes and the patch of sand was the boardwalk that Dante had crossed that August morning when Nadine had been looking for Bradley among the sea oats.

She could still see him, strong arms, strong voice, hip sunglasses, and as happy as he could be.

The last conversation she had with him was completely different. He had seemed downcast, dejected, run aground.

Almost hopeless.

"We're never hopeless in Christ," Nadine said.

"Is that a note to yourself, or are you thinking of a memory?"

"Maybe a bit of both." Nadine glanced over at

the terrace door to make sure it was closed. She didn't want Bradley to escape again.

"I thought you and my brother had a great time. He thought of you a lot."

And I, of him.

Still...

"Perhaps it's for the best. I only want God's will, Abilene."

"Even if it hurts?" Abilene produced a water bottle and sipped.

Nadine nodded.

Inside, she was in pain, but better to be in pain now than later, right? What if Dante turned out to be a cad later on in their relationship?

Uncle Ernest, for example, had been a gentleman until he married. In every single one of his three or four marriages, he'd had affairs. He'd married one of the other women, then dumped her for another. The cycle had continued until his sixties, when he stopped marrying altogether, and simply cohabited with last girlfriend.

To this day, years after Uncle Earnest had passed away, Nadine never quite figured out which ones of her six or seven cousins belonged to which mothers.

Yep. Better to break up now than later.

CHAPTER TWENTY-NINE

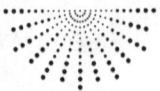

"What's wrong, Abilene?" Nadine was in her pajamas when she ushered Abilene into the small living room.

Abilene had driven all the way out to this side of Savannah, almost toward Richmond, to see Nadine for a reason.

"My brother. I'm afraid he's going to wither away."

Nadine's eyes grew big. Either Abilene's hormones were working overtime, or Dante was really in trouble.

Nadine felt a headache coming.

What should I do, Lord?

"Please sit down." Nadine cleared a space on a sofa. "Would you like something to drink?"

"Water, please. I was in such a hurry to come here that I left my water bottle at the gallery." Abilene eased onto the sofa and placed a palm on her tummy.

"I'll be right back," Nadine said.

In the kitchen, she stood over the faucet, a glass of water in her hand. She prayed again.

"Lord Jesus, please be with Dante. Whatever he is going through is never too difficult for You. Let him see Your mercy and grace today." Nadine drank the water meant for her friend. "Oops."

She found another clean glass and poured a new glass of water for Abilene.

"Thank you, Jesus, for keeping me calm. Show me what to do."

Back in the living room, Abilene drank the entire glass of water. Then she had to go to the bathroom.

Nadine sat there in her armchair, wondering when they'd ever get to the crux of the matter.

But Abilene was her friend. What concerned Abilene also concerned her, especially since it was regarding Dante.

Nadine remembered the summer before, when Abilene had called her from Simon's Gallery, crying, when she had thought that Lars had fathered a child out of wedlock.

Nadine had been Abilene's shoulder to cry on.

She was happy to be the sister that Abilene never had.

But on whose shoulders would Nadine cry if she had her heart broken?

Oh yeah, her heart was still broken, but she had kept it all in.

The only reason in the whole wide world that she was able to endure the abrupt breakup was the mercy of God.

The same thing she had told Dante in their last phone conversation was the advice she had to take herself.

Don't need me, Dante. Need Jesus.

Abilene returned to the living room with red eyes.

"Abilene." Nadine wrapped her arms around her and sat down with her on the sofa.

"I love my brother very much," Abilene said.

I love him too—

Nadine caught herself off guard with her own thoughts.

"So it hurts to see him suffer like that." Abilene sniffed. "He has resigned from Hot Dupree. He doesn't take calls. Doesn't talk to anyone."

"Sometimes people need space."

"Don't defend him, Nadine."

"Oh, okay. Go on."

"Thank you." Abilene sniffed again. "He sold

his shares to me. He would never give up his stocks in Hot Dupree. Ever."

"But he did."

"Exactly. Why is that?"

"His priorities changed?"

Abilene rolled her eyes. "Not Dante. He's always the persistent one, the go-getter, the high achiever. That's my brother."

"And now?"

"Now he's a loser. I told him to keep his shares, but Dad said that Dante could very well sell his shares to someone else if I don't buy them from him. The last thing we want is a non-Dupree owning one-fifth of Hot Dupree. That could kill Grandma, who is already in frail health."

"I'll pray for you." It was all Nadine could say.

"You know, that may be all we have."

"God is all we have, Abilene. God is all we have."

CHAPTER THIRTY

*N*o signal!

Nadine grunted her frustrations. She waved her iPhone up and down in front of her and then twirled it above her head. She walked here and there and then climbed on the picnic bench and table.

She stared into her iPhone, waving it like a magic wand.

It was no use.

Her iPhone was out. Her mobile hotspot modem didn't work either.

There is no signal in them thar mountain valleys.

"What are you doing?" Dad's eyebrows furrowed as he stuffed a chili dog into his mouth.

"Don't campgrounds have Wi-Fi?" Nadine sat

down on the table. She tapped the bench nervously with her hiking boots.

"Not this one."

"Why not?"

"Forty percent off doesn't come with Wi-Fi." The chili dripped out of the other end of Dad's hot dog, over the paper plate, and plopped onto the bare ground.

"Oh, I see. Let's get an upgrade. I'll pay."

"No, Nadine. This is Rusty's Rustic Retro RV Park. They do not have Wi-Fi."

"Let's move to one that does."

"Nope. I paid the whole sum. No refund."

Nadine's heart sank. "What about land lines at the main office?"

"You remember that place we stopped in Sevierville to pick up the keys this afternoon?" Dad asked.

"Yeah?"

"That's the main office." Dad wiped his mouth with an overused paper napkin. "The signals don't come into this valley."

"Did you do this on purpose, Dad?"

"Didn't you say you have the week off?"

"Yeah, but—"

"No buts, Nadine. If that college kid is covering for you, you don't have to worry."

"Yes, I do. Martin still needs me to tell him what's what."

"Oh well. I guess he's on his own then." Dad looked concerned. "Does he know what to do?"

"Yeah, he's very social media savvy. Can't write copy to save his life, but I've already taken care of anything related to writing."

"What's the worry?"

Nadine was so frustrated she couldn't speak.

"Control." Dad pointed a finger at her.

"What?"

"It's control. You want to do everything yourself."

"It's my company."

"You have just delegated, and you want it back."

Again, Nadine regretted that she had taken this trip with Dad.

She had only been trying to help.

Over the weekend, Dad had been sad again, weeping over Mom and what she might be doing in Cancun. On a whim, Nadine had suggested that they go camping like they used to when Nadine was in high school.

Sure, she could take the week off.

What had she been thinking, letting Dad do all the planning? Well, she had to do some last-minute work before giving instructions to Martin MacFarland, that college student she sometimes called to fill in for her whenever she had to be out of town.

Nadine had regretted it on Monday morning when they had packed Dad's Volkswagen camper van with picnic food and about half her kitchen.

She had no idea the campground didn't have Wi-Fi because she had left it to Dad to make the arrangements, and because she had assumed *all* campgrounds had Wi-Fi.

She had regretted it again that afternoon when they started driving away from Savannah and into the Georgia countryside, through beautiful fall foliage and small-town roads, then to South Carolina, crossing the border into the North Carolina side of the Great Smoky Mountains National Park, and all the way into this obscure valley in the middle of nowhere.

"We'll be back in Savannah by Sunday night," Dad said. "We only have four days to take father-daughter walks without any interruption."

Nadine's shoulders sagged.

"You agreed to camp with me until Saturday morning, and I agreed to go visit your friend in Sevierville that day and to go with y'all to her church on Sunday morning," Dad said.

Nadine was glad Dad remembered their plan.

She had emailed her friend to let her know they would be passing through Sevierville. Her friend had invited them to visit Mountain Chapel before they made the long drive home to Savannah.

She should be thankful that Dad had agreed to go with her.

Nadine watched Dad as he talked. He looked wearier as he got older. Mom was the one who had aged gracefully, often being mistaken for Nadine's older sister.

"If you don't take a break from your job, your job will break you," Dad said. "Guaranteed."

"What if one of us gets sick? How long would it take us to get to the nearest hospital?"

"We won't worry about that, all right?"

Worry?

Worried was when the bars on her iPhone had vanished one by one as they drove into the woods, passing by tall pine, tulip, gum, and other trees in the Great Smokies. After crossing a deep chasm on a rickety old bridge, Nadine's iPhone signal vanished.

No beeps. No messages. No emails.

Nadine had hoped that the signals would return when they reached the campground. If there had been an intermittent signal, she could have downloaded emails from her clients, and perhaps secretly worked at night after Dad had gone to bed in his tent.

He wouldn't have noticed. He would've been busy snoring.

"Do you need anything from the store?" Nadine hopped off the weathered pine bench.

"That dilapidated country store miles away?" Dad asked.

There was good signal there. She could download her emails, at the very least. "I'll drive."

"And how long will you be gone?"

"Not long." Nadine headed for the Volkswagen. This was a good time because they hadn't popped up the camper top or set up the awning yet. "I'll have to borrow your keys."

"No can do."

Nadine spun around. "Dad, please?"

Dad shook his head. "You promised."

"I didn't. I just said we could go camping. I didn't say I wasn't going to work."

"But God has another plan."

"God? I thought you don't believe in God." Nadine's shoulders dropped. It was bad posture, but she didn't care right now. She was behaving badly, but she needed to check her email!

"When He works in my favor, God's not too bad." Dad motioned for Nadine to go with him. "Come get some dinner. Don't want you to starve. Don't make me eat your hot dogs for you."

CHAPTER THIRTY-ONE

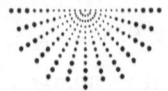

*N*adine sighed and turned off her iPhone. Might as well save the battery. What else could she do?

Then again, she had been so efficient as a virtual assistant that she had been all caught up before she arrived here. There were no files to edit, no calendars to sort, no due dates—

Dante.

"I have to call Dante." Nadine grabbed Dad's arm. "I told Abilene I would call today, and I haven't."

Truth was, she had been trying to forget Dante Dupree by keeping very busy. She had worked into the evenings. She had prayed and studied God's Word. She had started to memorize Scripture verses again to keep focused on God.

This camping trip was as much for her as it was for Dad.

"You kept putting it off," Dad said. "You didn't want to call him. I don't blame you. He dumped you and is now depressed. Serves him right for hurting my only daughter—"

"He didn't *hurt* me."

"Broke your heart."

That, he did. "He has issues to sort out."

"Don't defend him, Nadine."

Abilene said that too.

"I'm not defending him." Nadine sat down on one of Dad's camp chairs. It had duct tape here and there and a cup holder with a ripped bottom. It was probably one of Dad's garage sale finds.

"Who are you defending?" Mrs. McGill asked from several chairs away.

"Her ex-boyfriend," Dad said.

He helped, and didn't help.

"That can be tough." Mrs. McGill gave her an *I'm sorry* look.

Nadine said not a word.

There was nothing to say.

"Well, camping can be therapy."

"Thank you, Mrs. McGill."

"Susie."

"Susie." Nadine looked past their campground neighbor to the clusters of Winnebagos, Airstreams, and Volkswagen micro buses and campers parked like a circle of wagons around the campsite.

Beyond that, the clearing extended past a scattering of trees to the mountains beyond, autumn leaves of brilliant colors sweeping up the slopes. Nadine's eyes followed the tree line. Against the dusk, the last light of day hit the leaves and the tops of those trees all around the campsite.

The view was photograph worthy. Yellow, orange, and vermillion leaves shuffled in and out of green, maroon, and deep, deep red.

Bleeding heart red.

A paper plate with two hot dogs and fixings appeared under Nadine's nose. It was sloppily plated with slices of sweet pickles just thrown onto a splatter of chili and a clump of shredded cheese.

Nadine looked up.

"Eat." Dad motioned. On his faded gray sweatshirt was a streak of what looked like ketchup rubbed into the woven threads in his failed attempt to remove it.

Nadine glanced at her plate. Then at Dad again.

She choked up.

I've been very selfish.

"Thank you, Dad." Nadine forced herself to smile.

Dad looked up at the sky. "I was going to suggest

a walk after dinner, but it'll be dusk soon, and we'd best set up camp."

Nadine nodded. She and Dad had talked on the long day of driving here from Savannah. It should have taken only about six or seven hours, but they had to stop several times to let the VW engine cool off.

Anyway, the plan was that she would sleep inside the VW at night and Dad would sleep in a tent outside the door. He wanted to look up at the stars, he had said.

"Would you like to go for a walk after breakfast tomorrow?" Dad asked.

Nadine could barely speak. It was a request she could never refuse in their many years of camping out as a family. Only this time, Mom was absent.

She gulped. "I'd love to do that. Always."

"I wish your mom were here." Dad's voice was low. "She loves walks like this in the fall."

"We'll come back again next year, and I pray it'll be with her," Nadine said cheerfully. "How's that?"

"I like that idea. You pray to God about it, and ask Him to make it happen."

This was the second time Dad had brought up God in one day. Might God be working in his heart? What had she missed?

"I've been praying for Mom, and I'll add this to my prayer."

"You do that." Dad ambled away toward his grill.

Nadine saw him lift the base of his palm to his face. He didn't turn back to look at her.

Nadine closed her eyes and prayed for Dad's salvation, for Mom's return, for her parents' reconciliation, and then for the dinner that Dad had prepared for her.

Nadine logged into her iPhone and added the new prayer request to her long list.

Out of curiosity, she checked the bars.

No bars.

Zero signal strength.

Please, Lord, help me to walk by faith in You and not by signal—I mean, sight.

CHAPTER THIRTY-TWO

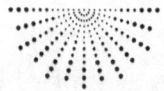

*A*s the leaves crunched beneath her hiking boots, Nadine was concerned that camouflaged snakes would launch out and bite her. She quickly stepped onto a worn dirt path.

Dad laughed at her imagination. "Remember when you were a little girl and we went out walking in the park near our house?"

"You mean the one where I spent half my time picking up sticks and stones?"

"Remember that time you used your stick to poke an ant hill and you were bitten all over by fire ants?"

Oh, that. Nadine groaned. "Great memories, Dad."

Dad laughed so hard his stomach jiggled.

Nadine could see the jiggling through his old sweatshirt.

She was happy that, for a moment, Dad wasn't sad. It had been a therapeutic camping trip thus far in the three days they had been here.

She had spent every waking moment with Dad, listening to him, talking shop with him about his salvage—also known as junk—business, reminiscing about Mom, and doing all those things that fathers and daughters would have done if they had the time.

And she had time.

Plenty of time.

Once Nadine had adjusted to being unplugged from the Internet, it didn't hurt too much. She had surrendered Saylor Virtual Services to her apprentice, Martin MacFarland, and had told him that he should contact Ming and Sabine if he encountered any emergency, in the event that she became unreachable. Ming Wei would find a way to track her down, if necessary.

So far, so good.

"We were a family then." Dad's voice was cracking again.

Here we go.

"We're still a family now." Nadine rubbed Dad's arm. "Happy thoughts of Mom are with us."

"Even though your mom is walking around in her swimsuit in Cancun?"

"You're jealous."

"What? No."

"She's still your wife."

Dad nodded. "I miss her, Nadine. I love her so much."

"Have you told her that?" Nadine asked.

"Told her what?"

"That you miss her and love her?" Nadine kept up with Dad's strides.

"Sure."

"Lately?"

"I don't recall."

Nadine laughed. "When you were in Cancun, did you tell her you love her?"

Dad held his head up. "She knows."

"Sometimes the obvious is not so obvious."

"Where did you learn all this kind of stuff?" Dad asked.

"From you and Mom, who else? And wisdom, I learn from God."

"God again." Dad's voice was quiet.

"God is the reason I'm not giving up on Mom."

"Your mom believes in Jesus," Dad said. "Why did she leave me? Doesn't the Bible have something to say about marriages and divorces?"

"Yes, it does. You two are separated, not divorced."

"It could come to that."

"But here's the point. Just because a Christian does something doesn't mean that it's approved or sanctioned by God."

Dad stopped in his tracks. "You mean your mother sinned against God?"

"Like they say, it takes two hands to clap," Nadine explained. "But my point is that we have a battle going on in our hearts and minds between right and wrong, good and best."

"Soledad isn't doing right?"

"Not the way I see it. And neither are you, Dad."

"Me? You're blaming me now?"

"Who am I to judge?" Nadine asked. "All I know is that if your marriage is in trouble, God can fix it. He sometimes sends counselors. You know that Pastor Samuel Flores—Pastor Flores's dad—is a marriage counselor at our church. He's been married fifty-some years. Maybe you could have a chat with him and let him show you some Bible verses that might be helpful."

Dad nodded.

"But first, God. Talk to God."

"About what, Nadine?"

Nadine rehearsed her words in her mind before she spoke. "Your relationship with Mom can't get right until your relationship with God is right. The Bible calls it an unequal yoke."

"Unequal what?" Dad stopped walking. Again!

If they kept stopping, it would be lunchtime before they returned to the campground. Still, Nadine felt that they had a lot to talk about, and this was the only time they could have some privacy. More Winnebagos and Volkswagen campers were rolling in.

"You two are not on the same page," Nadine explained. "Mom goes one way. You go another way."

"Yeah, but we're in the same bed and same house."

"Your hearts are not synced up."

"Sync? I get it. Same page."

"Right." Nadine nodded. "The more you love God, the more you'll love Mom."

"But all these church activities—I'm not sure I want to do them."

"Church activities come after you are right with God, right with Mom, right with your family. And that applies to Mom and me too."

There was more. Nadine prayed for wisdom to say the right words. She didn't want Dad to stop her from continuing to speak about God as he had done in the past.

"When Mom and I die, we'll go to heaven," Nadine said. "If you die, where do you go? Mom and I may never see you again."

"That would be bad."

"For you. I'll see Mom again. She'll see me. We want to see you again too, Dad."

Dad sighed. "What must I do to get to heaven?"

"Jesus Christ is your ticket. If you get Jesus, you get eternal life in heaven. And you also get peace in your heart, rest for your mind, and joy in your soul."

"I need peace in my heart."

"Jesus is my peace."

"Tell me what I must do."

"Do? Not *doing*, but *believing*. After all, Jesus has already done it all for us," Nadine said. "Man is sinful. God is holy. God sent Jesus to bridge the gap between God and us. Jesus died for my sins and saved me. Now I have a new heart in Christ, and I have a relationship with God. Do you want this new heart?"

"Yes, I do."

"Believe in the Lord Jesus, and you will be saved."

Pauses from Dad always made Nadine anxious. She waited.

Dad turned to her. "I believe."

"You believe? In the idea? In what I just said?"

"In Jesus," Dad said. "I now believe in Jesus."

CHAPTER THIRTY-THREE

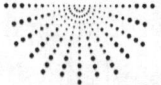

*T*he answer was still no.

Dante had called his physician one more time this morning and had received the same news.

Your spinal cord is never going to heal.

Dante hit the mattress on both sides of his body with his fists. "Why, God? Why?"

Mom walked into his bedroom. She smiled, like she had always done when Dante threw a tantrum. "He has something better for you."

"That's what preachers say, Mom."

"It's true." Mom kissed his forehead.

Her locks, once golden, now white, fell on Dante's cheeks, and he remembered when he had been a little boy running free in the backyard through sprays of water from the sprinklers. He had rolled in the wet grass with an equally wet beagle. All the while his eyes had been watching the porch where Mom sat knitting a pair of socks for him.

Those were the days.

Oscar the beagle had died a long time ago, as had Dante's carefree days.

All hopes of ever running through the backyard again had been vanquished.

When his parents grew old, would Dante be around to take care of them? Of Mom, especially?

"I might as well die," Dante barely whispered.

Mom was unfazed. She sat down at the edge of the bed and held Dante's hand. "We will all die someday. Until then, God has work for us to do."

"There's nothing for me, Mom. Nothing."

"Yes, there is." Mom patted his hand.

"Like what?"

"Stop fussing and God will tell you. Be still and know that God is God."

God is God. "I don't see what's left for me."

"See that? You said *see*." Mom smiled again.

The lines on Mom's face had deepened, but Dante still loved that smile.

"See what?" Dante asked. "I don't see."

"No? All you've done for a month is *see*, Dante. God wants us to walk by faith, not by sight, remember?"

That afternoon in August when Nadine

brought him chicken soup at Abilene's house, Nadine had said something like that to him.

You do know we don't walk by feelings but by faith.

Dante didn't feel like he had much faith right now.

"I have nothing to give her," Dante said.

Mom's eyes sparkled. "Oh? Is there a girl involved? Tell me more."

Dante groaned.

"What are you not giving her?" Mom patted his arm. "Come on. Talk."

Dante searched Mom's eyes.

Should I tell her?

"I'm listening, dear."

Cornered, Dante relented. "All right. I'm disabled."

"Not an excuse. What's her name?"

"Her who?"

"This woman whom you love."

Love?

"I can see it in your eyes," Mom said. "You're pining for her."

"I am?"

"You sure are."

Dante cleared his throat. "Did Abilene say something to you?"

"Nothing. You know me. I don't pry."

"No, you don't. That's what I love about you, Mom. You let us grow at our own pace."

"It's the Dupree way."

"Right."

"Out with it," Mom persisted.

Dante sighed. "She's better off with someone who can walk."

"Did you know her from high school?"

"No. Why?" Dante asked.

"That was when the football accident happened and you stopped walking."

"What are you getting at, Mom?"

"She met you when you were already in your wheelchair," Mom said. "Does she like you?"

"I think she loves me."

"And we've established that you love her."

"Too much." Dante pointed to his unmoving legs. "I have nothing to give her."

"Where is your heart?" Mom asked.

"You mean philosophically?"

"No. I mean where is it physically?" Mom pointed to Dante's chest. "Your heart is not in your legs, dear. You love from your heart, not from your legs."

Funny how it went. Dante remembered then what Nadine had said to him.

But you talked like your entire life is below the waist.

Nevertheless, Dante thought that he had done the right thing by Nadine. "I set her free, Mom."

"Did you? Or did you simply deny her what she wants: your love?"

"I, uh... My legs."

"Give her your love, dear, not your legs." Mom patted Dante's legs.

He could not feel his mother's touch. He wanted to weep.

"So what is it you cannot do? Cannot give? Who is it you cannot love? Cannot share your life with?" Mom's voice rose in a singsong way, her Welsh roots showing.

"You're a Dupree," she continued. "As long as you carry the Dupree name—with the help of God, of course—you can conquer the world."

"From a wheelchair?"

"Love conquers all, remember?"

Dante sighed.

"Does your torso belt still work?"

"Sure does." And then Dante remembered that afternoon in Savannah, the same afternoon Nadine had brought him chicken soup for his cold, when he had leaned too far forward to reach for a drink and almost fell out of his wheelchair.

Nadine had quickly placed her arm on his chest to prevent him from falling.

He could feel her touch now. He could still feel

the connection they had afterward when he had placed his hand on her wrist.

"Then what are we waiting for?" Mom asked. "It's only nine o'clock. Let's go, Son."

~

*D*ante Dupree had never been this antsy in his entire life. He thanked God that Mom had decided not to chaperone him. She had wanted badly to see Nadine Saylor in person, but Dante had managed to persuade her to change her mind about tagging along.

Here he was on this late Saturday afternoon, knocking at her front door as his wheels precariously perched on the makeshift ramp that Lloyd Saylor had somehow nailed to the sidewalk all the way to the door threshold.

Thoughtful man.

He rang the doorbell again several times. Then he turned his wheelchair around and went down the rickety ramp. It sounded like he was going down a luge track and that he, the luger, was missing a helmet. He wondered if the ramp was made to code.

He made it safely off the ramp and came to a stop a couple of feet in front of Waylon.

"Whoa." Waylon looked panic-stricken.

"Were you going to stop me with your entire body?" Dante chuckled.

"If I had to. I can take a hit."

"Glad we don't have to test that. Both of our health insurance costs could go up."

Dante transferred himself into the rental sedan on the passenger side. Waylon packed up the wheelchair and put it in the trunk.

"Where is she?" Dante asked. His stomach growled. It was nearly dinner time, but he had decided to wait so that he could rush out here to see Nadine.

"You know, sir, you normally check the details before you go to meet someone." Waylon climbed into the driver's side. "What happened this time?"

"I was in a hurry."

He hadn't decided to come back to Savannah until Mom's words rang clearer in his mind this morning. Then it had taken him about five hours to make it happen. The Gulfstream had to be refueled, the pilot paid extra for the last-minute flight, and his bags packed for the weekend trip.

Still, love conquers all, right?

It had been one of the longest months of his life, second only to that month after the accident on the football field so long ago. But his heart hurt more this time.

If he lost Nadine, it would be no one else's fault but his own.

"Where to, sir?" Waylon Diaz asked as he backed the car out of the driveway.

"To dinner. You and me."

"Very well, sir. And we can talk about our girl troubles."

"You too?" Dante's eyebrows rose.

"Me too. Any relationship advice for me?"

Dante nodded. "If you know she's the one, don't let her go. You may never get her back."

208

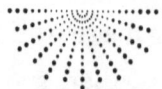

"*L*ike I said, if you had called me, I could have saved you a trip, big Brother."

Abilene took up her spot at the door to hand out programs for the Riverside Chapel Sunday morning church service.

Dante wheeled out of the way of the double doors so that people didn't have to walk around him. He appreciated the width the door opening because he was able to make a U-turn with ease, and his elbows didn't hit the doorframe when he turned the hand rims to get to Abilene's side.

His wheelchair took up space, a little bit more than his old one. The sports car of wheelchairs, its frame was made of titanium. It was light, strong, shiny, and could carry twice his weight.

Dante imagined Nadine sitting on his lap and

the two of them going down the boardwalk to watch the sunrise over the sands of Tybee Island...

"—help?"

Dante snapped back to reality. "Excuse me?"

"Would you like to help me hand out the programs?" Abilene asked.

"Are you putting me to work?"

"You're just sitting there staring into space."

"I wasn't exactly star—never mind. Sure. Give me a stack." Dante's palm stretched out, and he held the stack of programs Abilene gave to him. "Should I go to the other side of the door?"

"No. Stay here. Talk to me."

"Yes, ma'am."

Between handing out the programs, Abilene turned to Dante. "I'm so glad you came to church with us this morning."

"Me too. I'm getting back to attending more regularly."

"Glad to hear that. It's good for your soul, you know, to study God's Word."

"I know."

"What made you decide to get back to church?"

"I need God's leadership in my life." Dante handed out a program to an elderly gentleman who introduced himself as Melvin Theroux.

"We all need God's wisdom," Abilene said.

"Absolutely. It took me a while to realize that."

"Romans 8:28, Dante." Abilene smiled Mom's smile. "God works all things out for our good."

And we know that all things work together for good to those who love God, to those who are the called according to His purpose.

"That's right." Dante nodded. "I'm at church. And this is a good thing."

Abilene greeted an elderly lady she called Mrs. Untermeyer. "But it's not sacrifice that pleases God."

"Sacrifice?" Dante was puzzled.

"Of your time. This Sunday morning when you could have been sleeping in, big Brother, you chose to sacrifice sleep so you could come to church, even though Nadine is out of town."

"I would have come anyway because it's the right thing to do." Dante waited.

When Abilene didn't reply, Dante knew that his sister had more to say. "You're thinking of correcting me about something."

"No. I'm not scolding you. We'll leave that to Grandma, huh?" Abilene chuckled. "I meant to apply I Samuel 15:22, but I am doing it poorly."

"One sec." Dante swiped his iPhone. "Here's the verse."

So Samuel said:

*"Has the Lord as great delight in burnt offer-
ings and sacrifices,*

As in obeying the voice of the Lord?

Behold, to obey is better than sacrifice,

And to heed than the fat of rams."

"What do you want to say about it?" Dante
asked.

"God wants our obedience, not our sacrifice,"
Abilene said.

Dante nodded.

He had been trying to live his life on his own
since he had broken his back on the high school football field. Sure, he had finished college—magna cum
laude, to boot—and had worked his way up to this
point, on the verge of taking over as the new Hot
Dupree CEO.

Yet, none of that was enough.

Not enough. I want more.

I want God.

He had set aside God—the God who had saved
him in high school—so that he could try to make it
on his own. Now he ached to hear God's voice, to
hear Him speak to him once again.

And here, through Samuel and Abilene, even
before the eleven o'clock church service began, God
had spoken to him.

Forgive me, Lord, for my prodigal heart.

For sixteen years he had been running away from God in his speedy wheelchair, settling into a life he had chosen for himself, on his own, in his own mind, for his own purposes.

He had shunned God and had only attended church intermittently as a chore rather than as a desire to worship God with other believers.

It wasn't his wheelchair that had been the problem. He realized it now.

It was his heart.

His heart was more paralyzed than his legs.

Lord, I blamed You for taking away football from me.

I blamed You for taking away my legs.

He tried to keep his composure as he handed out the last program in his hands. At the other end of the dining room, the piano began to play "Amazing Grace."

Lord Jesus, now I surrender my legs to You. Use them for Your glory.

He could barely see through the mist covering his eye as he wheeled away from Abilene to reread I Samuel 15:22.

He had given quite a substantial amount to the building fund on behalf of Nadine, who had prevented Hot Dupree from getting into a merger disaster. The half a million dollars should bring the church closer to their goal of buying a property on land.

But here, on this riverboat, Abilene had told him of many lives changed for Christ, many downcast hearts encouraged, marriages restored, believers discipled.

A lot of things happened at this little church called Riverside Chapel.

Dante could easily give more money to the cause of Christ here.

Yes, even though he had sold his shares of Hot Dupree to Abilene during his worst moments, she had sold them all back to him, knowing how stupid he could sometimes be.

Yet God did not require of him the sacrifice of money. Money was nothing to Him. As it said in Psalm 50:10, God owned the cattle on a thousand hills.

For every beast of the forest is Mine,
    And the cattle on a thousand hills.

Instead, God wanted his obedience.

Quietly, Dante prayed.

Here I am, Lord Jesus. What is Your will for my life?

CHAPTER THIRTY-FIVE

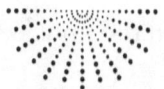

*N*adine crawled out of bed and padded to her bathroom with one eye opened. They had come home late the night before. It had been past midnight, as she recalled. Having had her internal clock reset by the week of camping, Nadine had been unable to stay up that late.

Dad had driven the rest of the way home to Savannah.

Nadine hardly remembered crawling into bed, much less changing into her pajamas.

She closed her eyes as she brushed her teeth.

Then she dragged herself toward the smell of bacon and eggs coming from her kitchen.

She barely reached the door of the kitchen when she saw him.

And froze.

She shrieked and ran across the living room and back into her bedroom, slamming the door behind her. She sat down on her bed, hands shaking. She fell back onto the bed, her palms covering her face for the longest time.

She barely heard the knocks on her door.

"Nadine?"

Keep cool. "Yes, Dad?"

"Someone would like to talk with you."

"I know."

What did he want? Why did he show up this early in the morning? Had he recovered from the doldrums? What had overcome Dad to cook breakfast for him?

"Get dressed, and come talk to him in the living room. Okay?"

"All right." *Oh, I'm so embarrassed.*

She got up from the bed, panicking. She had nothing decent to wear.

Absolutely nothing nice to wear.

But first, she had to take a long, hot shower.

"Your dad told me about his salvation." Dante watched Nadine sit down nervously at the end of the sofa, away from him on the other side of a scratched coffee table.

Nadine nodded. "It was something else. We were walking in the woods, talking about Mom, like we had done since we went up to camp, and God saved Dad."

"God is good."

"Always good."

"I heard it was beautiful up there in the mountains," Dante said.

Make small talk. Put her at ease. Reestablish the connection.

"It was," Nadine replied. "God is the ultimate Artist. You should've been—"

"There?" Dante asked. "I should've been there."

"Maybe next time," Nadine suggested. "Maybe you could go with Abilene and Lars."

"Or maybe I could with you."

"Me?"

Nadine's frown threw him off. Dante prayed for the right words to say.

"Nadine?" He managed to call her name.

"Yes?"

"There's this coffee table between you and me, and I can't get to you."

"I can hear you just fine."

Dante cleared his throat. "I'm sorry I was out of touch."

"Nothing to be sorry about. We broke up, remember?"

"We shouldn't have."

Nadine turned away to look out the window.

To Dante, she looked sad sitting there in her pretty purple turtleneck and stretch pants. How he longed to be able to sit next to her, to put his arm around her shoulder, to kiss away that sadness.

Mom's words came back to him.

So what is it you cannot do? Cannot give? Who is it you cannot love? Cannot share your life with?

"Nadine?"

She turned.

"Come here, please?"

Hesitantly, Nadine rose from the sofa. She walked to the other end of it and sat down. She was four or five feet away from Dante. "This is as far as I go."

There was still that coffee table...

"Fair enough." Dante wondered how to put his feelings into words. He had prepared his speech, but none of that seemed relevant to him now. All his grandiose words and proper grammar wouldn't work now, he realized.

He knew that Nadine wanted to hear his heart.

"I had to get past my disability," Dante explained. "My disability disabled me."

Nadine didn't respond one way or another. She didn't move a muscle, didn't speak, didn't do anything.

"It took time for me to learn to walk by faith in Jesus," Dante continued.

"We all have to walk—or live—by faith and not by sight."

"Me most of all."

"No. Me, most of all."

"Us both, then," Dante said.

"You mean *we* both."

"What?"

"We both have to live by faith and not by sight."

"What I said."

"No." Nadine shook her head. "You said *us. Us* both."

"Did not."

"I heard you loud and clear."

"Loudly and clearly?" Dante smiled.

It was Nadine's turn to wave him off. "Whatever."

"Well, since you have good ears, hear this. I love you, Nadine. I want to marry you, be the father of your kids—whether our own or adopted, however God provides. Will you marry me?"

Nadine broke into tears.

"Say yes."

Nadine was still sobbing. There was no way for Dante to reach her. The coffee table was a barrier to his wheelchair.

Nadine left the sofa and slid onto Dante's lap. She leaned against Dante's chest.

"You will outlive me, Nadine."

"What are you talking about?"

"You're going to have to raise our future children by yourself at some point."

"Don't speak like that," Nadine said.

"But I will make sure you won't have to do it alone."

"Stop." Nadine's tears were soaking his collar.

"Look at me." He rubbed her back and shoulders. "Will you marry me in spite of our difficult future?"

"Nothing is too difficult for God," Nadine reminded him.

Dante nodded. "Walking by sight focuses on the temporal, external, and man-made."

"Living by faith focuses on the eternal, internal, and God-made," Nadine added.

"Very good. So your answer is yes?"

"Of course."

"Even if I may have a short life?" Dante had to be sure.

"Every hair on our head is numbered, remember?" Nadine patted her pants pocket and frowned. "I left my phone in my room. Could you look up Matthew where it talks about that?"

"Sure." Dante swiped his iPhone. His Bible app was still open. He had been reading his Bible early this morning before he came out here to find Nadine. He typed in the reference.

"Here we go. Matthew 10:29-31. You read it." He handed his phone to Nadine.

Are not two sparrows sold for a copper coin? And not one of them falls to the ground apart from your Father's will. But the very hairs of your head are all numbered. Do not fear therefore; you are of more value than many sparrows.

Dante loved the sound of Nadine's voice reading the Bible. He hoped to hear it every morning for the rest of his life, however short or long.

My life is in God's hands.

Nadine searched for another verse. "Jesus gives life abundantly. John 10:10."

She found more. "Our lives are hidden with Christ. Colossians 3:3. Want other verses?"

"Are you preaching a sermon?"

Nadine typed in another search keyword into

Dante's Bible app and read the results. "Here's I John 5:12. If we have Jesus, we have life eternal."

She handed the iPhone back to Dante. "When our lives are over on Earth, we'll still see each other in heaven. And you'll be walking and running and sprinting. No patented, custom-made, gold-plated wheelchair to give you any advantage over the rest of us."

Dante chuckled. "It's not gold plated."

"Oh, you poor thing." Nadine looked straight into his eyes. "Yes, I'll marry you, Dante Dupree. God has put us together."

"Only you and me, Nadine." Dante's heart soared.

He tried to get to his pocket, but Nadine was in the way. She eased off his lap.

After fumbling the box with nervous fingers, Dante produced a sparkly engagement ring and slipped it onto Nadine's ring finger.

"Hmm... It fits," Nadine said.

"I had it resized."

"How did you—Dad!"

"What?" Dad hollered from the kitchen. "Three grandkids, please!"

Dante laughed with Nadine. "It wasn't your dad."

"Then who told you?"

"You and my sister share the same jeweler, remember? Abilene called him for me on Saturday."

"Should've guessed. Sneaky."

"There's no sneaking this." Dante tugged at her wrist, and another memory flooded his heart.

Nadine leaned down, reached his lips, and gave him a new memory to think about.

CHAPTER THIRTY-SIX

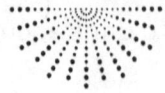

$\mathcal{N}$adine could barely concentrate on her work. Dad made such a loud din in the garage on the other side of her bedroom wall. How Nadine had agreed to turn the one-car garage into his workshop, she couldn't remember.

All she knew right now was that she could hear horrible metal-on-metal grinds and power tools and whatnots through her earplugs.

"That's it!" She pushed her chair back from the small table.

She marched all the way to the garage.

And there she was.

"Mom!" Nadine sprinted toward her and gave her a tearful hug. "I'm so glad you're home—I mean, here!"

"Cancun is overrated," Mom said.

"Figured," Dad said.

"Cancun feels different from what I remembered ten years ago," Mom continued.

"Without me?" Dad grinned.

"Don't know. Too hot. Too cold. Can't get the temperature right."

Dad stood up. "Sweetheart, it's my job to warm you up or cool you down."

Mom nodded. "You were MIA."

"Guess we could KAMU." Dad inched toward Mom.

Kiss and make up? Nadine rolled her eyes.

"Not in front of the children," Mom said.

"Child? We only have one."

"Not that we didn't try." Dad was standing next to Mom now.

Nadine felt like she was invading a private moment, but she had to know this wasn't a second or third goodbye. She remained standing there, off to one side, watching her parents' conversation.

"So what have you been doing, Lloyd?" Mom asked.

"Got saved and made you a baker's rack," Dad said, casual-like.

"You made me a—what did you say?"

"Baker's rack. Wanna see?"

"Before that. You got saved?" Mom's face changed.

"Yeah. I'll tell you all about it when we look at your new baker's rack."

"Sure. Let's go."

Arm in arm, they went out of the garage toward the toolshed that Dad had constructed in the back-yard, leaving Nadine standing there by herself, jaw down.

She closed her mouth.

Thank You, Lord! Now they can both be at my wedding together.

~

*I*t would be six months later before anyone could attend Nadine and Dante's wedding. The two of them had battled all that time to get their schedules to line up.

In the end, Nadine had given in and hired Martin MacFarland to work at Saylor Virtual Services for twenty hours a week. Previously, the college student had only been on call whenever Nadine was out of town.

With more time to plan her wedding, Nadine's stress level went down.

Mom had been the best help ever, being more

excited than Nadine over the wedding day. Nadine wasn't picky, so she let Mom do whatever she wanted as long as it was pretty and stayed within their budget.

When the first sprigs of azaleas and the first buds of daffodils and tulips bloomed through Savannah and Tybee Island, Nadine's and Dante's friends and families gathered in Abilene's backyard for the wedding ceremony by the Atlantic Ocean.

Before Nadine realized it, Pastor Flores was saying the closing words. "You may kiss the bride."

Nadine handed her bouquet to Abilene, her matron of honor, and left the chair she had been sitting on when they said their vows.

Gently, she sat on Dante's lap and wrapped her arms around his neck, as she usually had done. The simple, no-frills wedding dress cleared her knees in a modest way. The skirt flared just enough so that she could now sit comfortably on Dante's lap.

Nadine faced Dante and his ready lips.

He was smiling so much that, to Nadine, it looked like he could barely do anything else.

"You may kiss the bride," Pastor Flores repeated.

No response.

"Dante?" Pastor Flores raised his voice.

"Kiss the bride! Kiss the bride!" The wedding guests chanted in unison.

"Huh? Oh, yeah." Dante snapped out of his dream world.

Nadine laughed as he took her lips. The kiss was sweet and tasted like peppermint.

She decided that she would buy lots of peppermints for their future children, however many God might bring into their lives.

"We'll have to go down the aisle now," Dante said as they surfaced for air.

"So go." Nadine tucked her legs up under her A-line skirt that cleared the wheels.

"Ah, so that's why you bought this wedding dress." Dante wheeled them slowly down the short aisle to thunderous applause.

It was then that Nadine tuned in to the ocean beyond the boardwalk and the dunes. She glanced quickly at the sea oats where she and Dante had run into each other almost a year prior. She remembered their long conversation at the boardwalk.

It had been about Bradley the cat, currently napping upstairs in one of Abilene's guest bedrooms.

They had thought of letting Bradley out to mingle with the wedding guests, but the cat had been too contented sleeping on a bed to attend any wedding ceremony.

Along the aisle, Nadine waved to Mom and

Dad, sitting side by side and holding hands. Their fight was over—for now.

Thank You, Lord.

Nadine had invited her parents to live in her little house outside Savannah. She wasn't going to use the house much henceforth.

She and Dante were building a new house outside New Orleans for an easier commute to the Hot Dupree headquarters for him. Dante had considered building a branch in Savannah, but it meant being away from the heart of the company in Louisiana, near Grandma Dupree, the matriarch of the family.

As for Nadine, her job as a virtual assistant meant that she could work anywhere.

Nadine smiled at Ming and Sabine, and at Heidi sitting next to them. She nodded to Lars, happily holding a sleeping three-month-old Marguerite Kayla Cargill.

Nadine would have to get off Dante's lap as soon as they reached the end of the short aisle, but until then, she nestled her head on Dante's shoulder, smudging lipstick on his white collar.

She wasn't heavy, and the wheelchair could carry them both. Yet she didn't like to sit on Dante's lap too long because it put pressure on his legs.

Here. Time to get off and walk beside her husband.

Husband.

Wowee.

In her heart, Nadine thanked God a thousand times over for her marriage to someone she loved and who loved her, and for this wedding day, the first day of the rest of their lives together.

Love conquers all indeed.

DEAR READER:

Thank you for reading *Cherish You So* I hope you enjoyed the story of Dante and Nadine. The next book after *Cherish You So* in the Savannah Sweethearts collection is *Walk You There*, where old Savannah meets new Atlanta. Tour operator Tamsyn crosses path with builder Ryan in the city block where Tamsyn's family has lived for generations. Will fireworks fly?

Walk You There (Savannah Sweethearts Book 6)
JanThompson.com/walk

WELCOME TO SAVANNAH SWEETHEARTS

If *Cherish You So* is the first Savannah Sweethearts book you are reading, then welcome to the series!

Savannah Sweethearts begins with *Ask You Later*, where readers are introduced to Riverside Chapel in downtown Savannah, Georgia.

Ask You Later (Savannah Sweethearts Book 1)
JanThompson.com/ask

READ A FREE EBOOK!

Set in Georgia, South Carolina, and Tennessee, this Christian romance tells the story of art gallery archivist Sheryl Breckenridge and world-famous sculptor Winton Pace.

Time for Me (A Vacation Sweethearts Prequel)
JanThompson.com/time-free

JOIN MY BOOK NEWS MAILING LIST

Subscribe to my newsletter to receive book news updates and special book sales. Be notified when my new books are available.

Jan Thompson's Mailing List:
JanThompson.com/newsletter

PLEASE LEAVE A REVIEW

If you'd like to leave a review for *Cherish You So,* please follow this link to your favorite retailers to leave your honest opinion about the novel.

Cherish You So (Savannah Sweethearts Book 5)
JanThompson.com/cherish

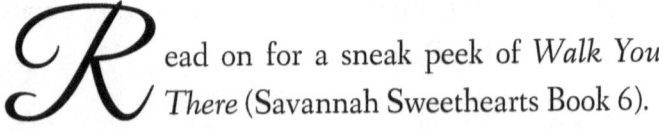ead on for a sneak peek of *Walk You There* (Savannah Sweethearts Book 6).

THE NEXT BOOK IS WALK YOU THERE

SAVANNAH SWEETHEARTS BOOK 6

She wants to save history. He wants to raze it all.

A local tour guide who makes a living off Savannah history goes to battle against an award-winning developer who wants to demolish the old city block she lives on.

TAMSYN'S TROUBLES...

Tamsyn Pendegrast's troubles can be summed up in one word: Ryan.

Okay, three words: Ryan Ruttledge V.

A nightmare to her historical preservation efforts, an enemy of her fledgling Tamsyn Tours travel agency and tour company, Ryan seems to have it all: funding, support, awards, and the deeds to half the properties on Rosa Pendegrast Lane in old-town Savannah. Only three historic homes remain unsold. One of them is the Pendegrast family home where Tamsyn has lived since she was a baby.

Savannah residents will not take this destruction sitting down. Tamsyn is sure of it. No way will they let Ruttledge Yamada Urquhart Commercial Properties turn her nineteenth-century city block into a ghastly sprawl of glass-and-steel sculpture. It's Tamsyn's duty to Savannah history and to the memory of the Pendegrast family to educate that Ryan dude on why he should just leave the past alone.

There. Her task is set.

If only he wasn't so charming...

RYAN'S RUCKUS...

Three more houses to buy, and the city block will belong to Ryan's commercial property company. Then he will reshape the area into a modernist architectural creation. One more award to win, and one more plaque to hang on the wall of his Atlanta office. Easy peasy, right?

All he has to do is get past Tamsyn Pendegrast. That small-town tour guide has a property he wants. One house. How hard can it be to get one house? If she sells her ramshackle old house, her two neighbors will follow.

Why is she holding out? His company has offered Tamsyn three times the value of her property. That worn and weary Queen Anne style Victorian house isn't going to last through the twenty-first century, anyway. Its foundation has been reinforced twice, and no amount of paint will restore it to its old glory. Tamsyn is simply holding on to a past that cannot be regained. She might as well give it up.

And yet, Tamsyn's tenacity intrigues him. It's messing with his mind.

And heart.

Uh-oh.

Walk You There (Savannah Sweethearts Book 6)
JanThompson.com/walk

Savannah Sweethearts
JanThompson.com/savannah

Jan Thompson's Book News Mailing List:
JanThompson.com/newsletter

WALK YOU THERE CHAPTER 1
SNEAK PEEK

"Tamsyn Tours. How may I help you?"

The sweet, euphonious voice filled Ryan Ruttledge's ears. He blinked. His talking points were at the tip of his tongue, but now they had vaporized.

What did I say her voice was?

"Hello?"

"Um... Is that Tamsyn Pendegrast?" Ryan asked.

Um? Was that the best he could do?

Silence.

"This is Ryan Ruttledge. May I speak with Tamsyn?"

More silence.

"Hello?" Ryan tried again.

Click.

Actually, it sounded more like someone had just thrown her cell phone across the room, but then again, that couldn't possibly be the case since the Tamsyn he had interacted with via emails, phone calls, and videoconferences the previous few months seemed to have a sweet, smiling nature— except when he had infuriated her.

Which had been about once in every conversation.

More so in the two weeks since Ruttledge Yamada Urquhart Commercial Properties had purchased half the rundown city block where Tamsyn lived in old-town Savannah.

On the phone a minute before, she had seemed to be back to her sweet self before she found out it was him on the other end of the line. He had his caller ID blocked, but the moment he had spoken, she had reacted.

Until then, her voice had been soothing to hear.

Euphonious—

Uh, did I say euphonious?

Ryan frowned. He couldn't remember the last time he used that word to describe a woman's voice on the phone.

He growled. "No one hangs up on Ryan Ruttledge V."

Across the room, between two large display tables featuring the talents of RYUCP, his business partner laughed like a hyena.

"Not helping, Hiroki." Ryan sank into his two-thousand-dollar task chair. He crossed his feet at the edge of the table.

"Last I checked, plenty of women hung up on Ryan Ruttledge V," Hiroki continued.

"Not when I'm offering them a sweet deal."

"Sweet? You want to raze her precious city block down to the ground and build a glass tower. That's not sweet to some people."

"It's a great deal. It'll revitalize that entire area," Ryan reasoned, almost to himself, but more so as a rehearsal to present to the people of Savannah. "I want that city block."

"She's in the way."

"She and that Save Old Savannah group of theirs. Who funds them anyway?" Ryan crossed the plush carpet to his cappuccino machine.

Hiroki Yamada was on it, swiping here and there on his iPad. "Mostly they themselves and local residents, perhaps. No famous families listed—wait! I spoke too soon. Here are a couple. Cavanaugh. Matheson. Old money."

"I'm not familiar with those names," Ryan said. "What about her own family? What are we up against?"

"Pendegrast? Not much information about them. We do know that Jerome Pendegrast owns two riverboats. He donated one to a church a while back."

"Riverside Chapel or something." Ryan made himself a small cup of hot cappuccino. "Want a cup?"

"Nope. Had too much today." Hiroki grinned. "Wouldn't Satan revel in the day that two Christians fight each other to the death over a bunch of dilapidated nineteenth-century buildings."

Ryan bristled. "Tamsyn and I are not *fighting* per se. We just have a disagreement—uh, many disagreements."

He was lifting the cup to his lips when it came loose from his fingers. The hot liquid splashed on his hand. He yowled.

Now there was a dark, hot mess on the camel-colored carpet in the open office.

Hiroki was on it with gobs of paper napkins.

"No, no." Ryan told him to get up. "My mess, my cleanup. Go compile the lowdown on the

Pendegrast family. Something I can use to get Tamsyn on my side. She's the only one standing between me and our next architectural award."

"Just so you know, I've never been one for awards," Hiroki said.

"I know. You love the work. The work is its own reward, blah, blah."

Hiroki handed Ryan more paper napkins and walked back to his workstation in the big room. "Do you want me to call housekeeping?"

"Later. I don't want them in here right now while I'm plotting the demise of Tamsyn Tours." Ryan dabbed the carpet. The patches of spilled coffee were still somewhat dark.

He made himself a fresh cup of cappuccino.

"How hard can it be?" Ryan asked no one. "They're just a bunch of no-name tour guides."

"Tour guides with backing from the Savannah people and some well-to-do families," Hiroki reminded him. "Old money dating all the way back to Charleston, in the days when it was known as Charles Towne."

"Was it?" Ryan sat down, savoring his caffeine. He had flunked American history in college but managed to pass the third time he had taken the class. It had helped that he had an easygoing teacher in the summer.

Hiroki nodded. "Don't mess with old money, is all I can say. They have staying power."

"Money can run out."

"That too."

"Seriously, she can't be that hard to knock down." Ryan logged into his laptop and browsed through the Tamsyn Tours website. "She's a small fry."

"Why did you say that?"

"She answered her own phone. Control freak."

"How do you know she's a control freak?" Hiroki asked. "Have you ever met her?"

"No, but all those videoconferences—"

"They mean nothing. You need to meet her in person."

"But all signs point to that. Her pretty voice, the way she sounds so pleasant on the speakerphone. All for show."

"You don't believe that."

Sweet.

Euphonious.

Noooo... I will not fall for that.

Hiroki spun around in his task chair. "There's only one thing to do, Ryan, old friend."

"What?" At this point, Ryan was out of options.

"You have to take a vacation in Savannah."

"Whatever for? I can buy that city block from here."

"But in your ivory tower, you can't see what the little people want."

Little people?

"The peasants." Ryan began to get it.

"When you're on the ground, you can find out what the fuss is about. You know, why she's been hating you for the last two months or more."

"Might be something I said."

"You think?"

Ryan brushed him off. He warmed up to the idea of a vacation on the coast of Georgia. It was April, and the weather would be nice. He could take a walk among the azaleas and get some photographs of those flowers his mother loved.

He had been so busy lately that he hadn't gotten back to his photography hobby. With Savannah's collection of architecture, there should be plenty of buildings to photograph and to identify for a buyout.

It would be a change of scenery for him from this landlocked Buckhead office.

Ryan sighed. "I hate that woman."

"But you'd love to have that corner property," Hiroki countered.

"Yeah. You'd think by the way she's taking this so personally that she's protecting her family farm."

"She is. That house has been in her family since

the late nineteenth century. The road was renamed after her great-grandmother, remember?"

Rosa Pendegrast Lane.

"She's not going to give it up," Ryan concluded.

"Conceding already?" Hiroki laughed. "Face her like a man, Ryan."

"What did you say?"

"You heard me. We've been business partners for a long time, and you know I speak the truth." Hiroki waved his iPad in Ryan's face. "There's a public meeting tonight at seven o'clock at the riverboat. Just be sure to go to the right riverboat. Not Riverside Chapel. The other one. It's called—"

"I have to work tomorrow."

"I'll cover for you. Nothing happens on Fridays around here anyway. Take a long weekend off."

"You think I should attend the meeting," Ryan said.

"Especially when one meme she posted to social media says, 'Stand Up Against Ruttledge Yamada Urquhart, Savannah History's Nightmare.'"

"It says that? Let me see." Ryan motioned for Hiroki to hand him his iPad.

"Ah, she's taking it personally." The other memes in the series said worse things about Ryan. "I could sue her for defamation."

"One block of ramshackle buildings," Hiroki said, refocusing Ryan's thoughts.

Ryan nodded. "Yeah. How hard can it be to knock them down?"

How hard can it be to get past sweet Tamsyn?

Sweet?

Did I say sweet?

What's wrong with me?

Walk You There (Savannah Sweethearts 6):
JanThompson.com/walk

More Information about Savannah Sweethearts:
JanThompson.com/savannah

To keep up with Jan Thompson's book news:
JanThompson.com/newsletter

READ A FREE EBOOK IN THE SAME STORY WORLD

Set in Georgia, South Carolina, and Tennessee, this clean and wholesome Christian romance tells the story of art gallery archivist Sheryl Breckenridge and world-famous sculptor Winton Pace. Read this ebook for free!

Time for Me (A Vacation Sweethearts Prequel)

JanThompson.com/time-free

ACKNOWLEDGMENTS

Many thanks to my Georgia Press publishing team for keeping up with my writing schedule.

For this book, I thank my outstanding copyeditor, Dori Harrell, and my patient proofreader, Lenda Selph. Their eyes for details are from the Lord.

I also want to thank my husband and son for their constant support and encouragement. And my parents for instilling in me the love to read and write at a very early age.

I am grateful to God for my husband and son for their support and encouragement. I also thank God for my parents and my three brothers for my happy and memorable childhood. I'll always remember my beloved mother and my late father for having instilled in me the love of reading and writing from a very early age. I miss my father here on earth, but I will see him again in heaven someday.

Most of all, I am eternally thankful to my Lord and Savior, Jesus Christ, who died on the cross to save me from my sins and rose again from the grave to give me eternal life. Without Him, I can write nothing (John 15:5).

Jan Thompson
John 3:16

BOOKS BY JAN THOMPSON

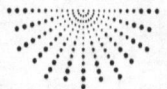

CONTEMPORARY CHRISTIAN CITY, COASTAL, AND BEACH ROMANCE

Seaside Chapel (7 Books)
JanThompson.com/seaside
Savannah Sweethearts (12 Books)
JanThompson.com/savannah
Vacation Sweethearts (8 Books)
JanThompson.com/vacation

CHRISTIAN ROMANTIC SUSPENSE AND NEAR-FUTURE TECHNOTHRILLERS

Protector Sweethearts (6 Books)

JanThompson.com/protector
Defender Sweethearts (6 Books)
JanThompson.com/defender
Binary Hackers (4 Books)
JanThompson.com/binary

Subscribe to Jan Thompson's mailing list:
JanThompson.com/newsletter

SEASIDE CHAPEL

Welcome to *USA Today* bestselling author Jan Thompson's Seaside Chapel Christian beach romance series. These novels are set on real-life St. Simon's Island, Georgia—a beach town where history is all around and the future is a moment away—and the neighboring fictitious Seaside Island, where the rich and famous live.

Savor the small-town atmosphere and the warm southern beaches of St. Simon's Island and the idyllic Golden Isles along the Atlantic Ocean. Enjoy the music of the orchestra and hymns of the church, and hang out with our Christian friends who attend Seaside Chapel, a little church by the sea known for its beach weddings and fair share of love and life.

As these Christians grow in their knowledge and understanding of God, they are tested in their spiritual maturity, their love lives, and their relationships with others. Share their heartaches and healing, and cheer them on as they celebrate faith, family, and friends.

- Book 0 (Prequel): *His Surprise Proposal*
- Book 1: *His Longing Heart*
- Book 2: *His Wake-Up Call*
- Book 3: *His Morning Kiss*
- Book 4: *His Quiet Serenade*
- Book 5: *His Waiting Love*
- Book 6: *His Beach Retreat*

For more information about Seaside Chapel:
JanThompson.com/seaside

SAVANNAH SWEETHEARTS

Welcome to the new south! From *USA Today* bestselling author Jan Thompson come these clean and wholesome, sweet and inspirational Christian romances set on the romantic beaches of Tybee Island and in the coastal town of Savannah, Georgia. Meet a group of multiracial and multiethnic churchgoing Christians who love the Lord, work hard in their careers, and seek God's will for their love lives. Against a backdrop of ocean, sand, and sun, these inspirational romances showcase aspects of the human need for God and for one another. Have some tea, settle in a comfortable reading chair, and enjoy these sweet celebrations of faith, hope, and love in Jesus Christ.

- Book 1: *Ask You Later* (Artist Romance)

- Book 2: *Know You More* (Multiracial Romance)
- Book 3: *Tell You Soon* (Asian-American Romance with Suspense)
- Book 4: *Draw You Near* (International Romance)
- Book 5: *Cherish You So* (Wheelchair Billionaire Romance)
- Book 6: *Walk You There* (Old-Meets-New Tour Guide Romance)
- Book 7: *Love You Always* (Romance with Suspense)
- Book 8: *Kiss You Now* (Multiracial Romance)
- Book 9: *Find You Again* (Multiracial Romance)
- Book 10: *Wish You Joy* (Christmas-Themed Romance)
- Book 11: *Call You Home* (Deaf Chef Romance)
- Book 12: *Let You Go* (Asian-American Romance with Suspense)

For more information about Savannah Sweethearts:
JanThompson.com/savannah

VACATION SWEETHEARTS

Travel with our friends from Savannah, Georgia, to the coast and to the mountains. Cheer them on as they celebrate the immeasurable grace and undeserved mercy of God through Jesus Christ.

The Vacation Sweethearts novels are a spin-off of Jan's Savannah Sweethearts series, and fans will recognize familiar faces from Riverside Chapel, a church in the coastal city of Savannah, Georgia. In fact, we might even visit the beach town of Tybee Island from time to time to visit old friends and beloved families...

- Book 0 (Prequel): *Time for Me*
- Book 1: *Smile for Me* (International Romance)

- Book 2: *Reach for Me* (Romance with Suspense)
- Book 3: *Wait for Me* (Romance with Suspense)
- Book 4: *Look for Me* (Romance with Suspense)
- Book 5: *Pray for Me* (International Romance)
- Book 6: *Care for Me* (Small Mountain Town Romance)
- Book 7: *Cheer for Me* (International Romance)

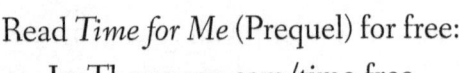

Read *Time for Me* (Prequel) for free:
JanThompson.com/time-free

For more information about Vacation Sweethearts:
JanThompson.com/vacation

PROTECTOR SWEETHEARTS

Private investigator Helen Hu and her associates specialize in searching for missing persons and hunting for lost treasures. Join them in their adventure suspense around the world in *USA Today* bestselling author Jan Thompson's Protector Sweethearts, a series of Christian Romantic Suspense with a side of mystery.

Protector Sweethearts is a spin-off of Savannah Sweethearts and Vacation Sweethearts.

- Book 1: *Once a Thief*
- Book 2: *Once a Hero*
- Book 3: *Once a Spy*
- Book 4: *Twice a Fighter*
- Book 5: *Twice a Convict*
- Book 6: *Twice a Soldier*

For more information about Protector Sweethearts:
JanThompson.com/protector

DEFENDER SWEETHEARTS

Defender Sweethearts is a sister series to the Protector Sweethearts Christian romantic suspense collection. While the heroes in Protector Sweethearts search for lost treasures and lost people, the Defender Sweethearts novels focus on protecting the helpless and hopeless. The main characters in Defender Sweethearts come from the supporting cast in Protector Sweethearts.

- Book 1: *Never a Traitor*
- Book 2: *Never a Hostage*
- Book 3: *Never a Fugitive*
- Book 4: *Always a Maverick*
- Book 5: *Always a Champion*
- Book 6: *Always a Guardian*

For more information about Defender Sweethearts:
JanThompson.com/defender

BINARY HACKERS

Like more suspense with your Christian romance? Like to read suspense thrillers? If you're looking for clean near-future romantic suspense without compromising the Christian faith, these books are for you.

From *USA Today* bestselling author Jan Thompson come these inspirational near-future cyberthrillers combining technothriller and romance, starting with Binary Hackers that feature computer specialists living at the edge of cyber-space, where they have to juggle being law-abiding truth-telling Christians while carrying out their assignments by any and all means possible.

The Binary Hackers series is set in the same story world as Jan's other books, and characters from the other series may make cameo appearances in this series and vice versa.

- Book 1: *Zero Sum*
- Book 2: *Zero Day*
- Book 3: *Zero Base*
- Book 4: *Zero Trust*

For more information about Binary Hackers:
JanThompson.com/binary

ABOUT JAN THOMPSON

USA Today bestselling author Jan Thompson writes clean and wholesome contemporary Christian romance with elements of women's fiction, Christian romantic suspense with an air of mystery, and inspirational international thrillers with threads of sweet Christian romance. Jan's books are for readers who love inspiring stories of faith, hope, and love in Jesus Christ.

Raised on a tropical island in the eastern hemisphere, Jan now lives and writes in the western hemisphere. Her international background gives her a unique multicultural and multiracial perspective to her novels and books. The island has never left her, and she reminisces about beach life in her beach romance novels.

When Jan is not busy writing small-town stories, she writes big-city romantic suspense and international technothrillers, a nod to her previous career in computer science. She weaves technology with human interests, reflecting the current and future digital world. And romance. There's always romance.

Beyond the printed page, Jan is a wife, mother, family scribe, avid reader, occasional artist, erstwhile pianist, and chief of staff to the family cat.

Find out more about Jan Thompson:
JanThompson.com

Subscribe to Jan's book news mailing list:
JanThompson.com/newsletter

For God so loved the world,
that He gave His only begotten Son,
that whosoever believeth in Him should not perish,
but have everlasting life.

—John 3:16